THE GUARDIAN OAK

~

The Call of Ancient Spirits
Volume II

by

R.L. Mannings

The Guardian Oak
Text Copyright
© 2023 R.L. Mannings
All Rights Reserved

R.L. Mannings has asserted the right to be identified as the author of this work in accordance with the Copyright, Designs and Patents Act 1988.
No reproduction, copy or transmission of this publication may be made without written permission. No paragraph of this publication may be reproduced, copied or transmitted save with the written permission of the publisher, or in accordance with the provisions of the Copyright Act 1956 (as amended).

This is a work of fiction. All of the characters, places, organisations and events portrayed in this story are creations from the author's imagination or used fictitiously.

British Library Cataloguing-In-Publication Data
A catalogue record of this book is available from the British Library.

ISBN 978-1-7394977-0-5

Cover Design by dartworks.design
Cover Illustration by Pete Blayney
Published via pgprintandofficeservices.co.uk

Acknowledgements

Thanks to my first readers for their support and enthusiasm especially...

Karl Mannings, and Andy and Maggie Wilkes.

Special thanks to Anne who offered valuable advice.

Finally, my thanks to Paula Good whose skills and kind forbearance have been invaluable in getting this project into print.

Contents

Prelude I
Chapter 1 1
Chapter 2 5
Chapter 3 11
Chapter 4 14
Chapter 5 20
Chapter 6 23
Chapter 7 26
Chapter 8 30
Chapter 9 33
Chapter 10 36
Chapter 11 38
Chapter 12 42
Chapter 13 48
Chapter 14 57
Chapter 15 62
Chapter 16 67
Chapter 17 70
Chapter 18 76
Chapter 19 81
Chapter 20 90
Chapter 21 93
Chapter 22 100
Chapter 23 105
Chapter 24 107

Chapter 25	109
Chapter 26	117
Chapter 27	123
Chapter 28	131
Chapter 29	137
Chapter 30	144
Chapter 31	146
Chapter 32	152
Chapter 33	156
Chapter 34	161
Chapter 35	165
Chapter 36	168
Chapter 37	172
Chapter 38	177
Chapter 39	183
Chapter 40	188
Chapter 41	195
Chapter 42	202
Chapter 43	208
Chapter 44	214
Chapter 45	216
Chapter 46	218
Chapter 47	221
Chapter 48	225
Chapter 49	229
Chapter 50	232

The Pixsan are facing new challenges in their struggle against the earth spirit Cernounos.

Cernounos feeds on human grief and, to grow, must upset the natural balance between grief and the joy of living. During the escape of Cernounos from his long imprisonment in Capstone Hill, the Pixsan managed to return him to his previous state as a simple earth spirit. However, he remains a danger. To feed his addiction to grief, he ferments conflict between humans wherever he can. To do so, he has begun to corrupt and recruit rich and powerful allies.

For years, the secretive Pixsan have kept themselves isolated and apart from society for fear of persecution. The actions of Cernounos have forced them to intervene.

Prelude

Narsin looked across at Rosa. Despite the hard work of the last three years, she had not changed.

"Narsin, wake up!"

Narsin stirred from his daydream. They had wandered up to the lone oak above the woodland, and were sitting in the dappled light beneath its shady branches. They were both tired — teaching the constant stream of young Resistants the Tort Mae had been sending to the farm was taking its toll.

The old Refuge at the top of the valley had been converted into a place of study. It now housed thirty student guest rooms and teaching facilities where the Resistants could practise their developing skills. Since the day it had opened, every place had been full. Teaching them had been rewarding, but also exhausting.

Experienced Pixsan came from other communities to teach students who shared their abilities, but they only stayed as long as they were needed. The brunt of the work fell on Narsin and Rosa. Meldrum the Elder only came when Wilds were brought in. There were more of these now and nobody truly knew why. Talent rarely manifested itself before the mid-teen years. Youngsters with varying degrees of it were appearing in towns and villages nearby and in the city to the north.

Talent was an impossible thing to grasp for the non Pixsan. It was often diagnosed as a mental illness and treated with drugs. Those with a minor talent were often afraid to talk about it. They tended to self-medicate with alcohol. For these Wilds there was little hope. If the Pixsan could get to a Wild in time she or he would be offered sanctuary or normality.

There were a few amongst the Pixsan who could remove Talent, but it was always a last resort. The girls had a tendency to be stronger and mostly chose sanctuary. A surprising amount of the boys chose normality. Meldrum the Elder dealt with those.

Some were very strong in the Talent and could see dark shapes in the sea or hear voices from trees and rivers. They were often considered crazy by their families and friends. Sadly, they came to believe themselves to be insane and eventually ended up with serious mental illness.

The Pixsan travelled to local towns for the things they could not make or grow. When they did, they kept a look out for Wilds.

Cernounos the Trickster had not been seen or heard of since his diminishing, but all knew he would return. The Trickster was like a virus. It needed to feed off human grief and ferment the violence that would cause it. If human grief and joy stayed in its natural balance he could not grow.

The Trickster was an earth spirit. The violence and hatred he fermented would lead to the destruction of the green world where spirits prospered. In feeding himself, he was destroying the world for human and spirit alike, but his compulsion would not let him stop.

Cernounos was weak now and could not travel far. He would have to start by causing grief locally. The whole of the Pixsan community constantly monitored news and gossip for anything that looked like his work. Rosa and Narsin thought that the increase in Wilds was connected in some way to the return of Cernounos, but they did not know how or why.

"Come, Narsin, Charly and Corrin will soon be at the farm, and we need to meet with the others to hear of their progress."

Narsin stirred himself.

Charly and Corrin had begun a new venture. The Tort Mae had discovered an old hotel on the north coast located between Ilfracombe and Lynton. It had been built in a Swiss timber-framed style at the bottom of a steep wooded combe by wealthy Victorians. It was in a state of very bad repair, but the Tort Mae saw a future for it in the project to reconnect the Pixsan with the sea. It was purchased with some surrounding farmland to make it as elusive as all Pixsan dwellings. They had already established a community, and built a complex into one side of the narrow combe. The next challenge was to build a pier. The plan was to construct an ocean-going sailing ship.

When they arrived at the farm, they headed straight for the meal room. Rosa and Narsin took seats at the head of the table next to Meldrum the Elder and Konia. Charly and Corrin were at the foot of the table where honoured guests were always seated. Rosa spoke the grace of her faith and Corrin was asked and spoke the grace of the Pixsan.

The aroma of roast lamb preceded the old men who brought food to the table. When all were finished, and more mead wine was brought, everyone made their reports. The farm was flourishing. Crops and animals were doing well. Rosa talked of the skill college. Now that Josie and Anna had returned from Spain she hoped that Narsin and she could get a little respite. Josie and Anna had grown much on their travels and were full of what they had learnt from the family Malarta. They were ready to take on teaching now.

Charly spoke of the House of the Mer. The hotel had finally been restored and a new Pixsan complex had been built on the left side of the combe. Some dwellings were built into the cliff face. In front of these was a courtyard and square surrounded by more dwellings and community buildings. It offered protection against the strongest winds from the north and the highest spring tide.

The next step was to build a workshop. A place where they could design the pier, and eventually the sailing ship. They had designated an area on the right side of the combe as they knew some metal machinery would be needed. The few Sensitives who chose to live there would be as far away as possible from the metal that dulled their connection with the land.

Now what was needed were the skills. No one in the Pixsan community had experience of pier- or ship-building. Their carpentry was of mortice and tenon or dowel, rather than screw or nail. Rosa was thinking about the problems the Mer family faced and thought she had an answer. She would speak to Corrin and Charly later.

Rosa had the feeling she had been missing something all evening. When she asked Narsin, he agreed that something was going on. She was sure Charly and Corrin had been suppressing their excitement about something, but they talked of nothing new in their report. Corrin was normally easy to read, but tonight he was making an effort not to be.

Just as the evening was about to end, a Sparrow hawk flew in from the open doorway, dropped a note into Rosa's lap, then flew towards Charly and perched on her shoulder. Rosa opened it and handed it to Narsin, who read it and passed it to Meldrum the Elder. True to tradition, the old woman stood.

"The Pixsan are blessed, for a new child comes to us. Congratulations, House of the Mer, may your child bring you happiness." All stood and raised their glasses to the foot of the table.

Charly and Corrin smiled, knowing they were bringing their child into a family wherein all would care for it and love it as their own.

CHAPTER 1

Josie and Anna had taken over some of the training, so Rosa and Narsin allowed themselves time off during the week. Sundays were family days. This was when neighbouring communities visited each other. For the heads of families, these were as much business meetings as family visits, so while the others socialised and the youngsters played together, Narsin and Rosa were working.

Each family had a product or two unique to them. Exchange rates had to be agreed and transport organised. Sometimes, if a community had nothing to offer, labour was sent in the form of skills the receiving community lacked.

A day off in the week seemed inviting but, in truth, they would be out on yet more Pixsan business. Rosa was a minor Talent sensitive; she could feel when people were gifted. Narsin suggested that they use the time to visit surrounding towns in search of Wilds.

~

After first-meal, on their first day off, they walked across the valley to the old barn where Rosa kept her car. They had decided they would drive over the moor, through South Molton and across to the Taw Valley road. They passed through Witheridge, Black Dog and other villages and hamlets, but Rosa felt nothing.

When they arrived in Crediton, they were quite hungry. They left their car in Parliament Street and went to see if food was being served at the Three Hogs Inn on the Town Square.

The Inn had a long history and was once a coaching inn for those travelling to Exeter from the North of the country. The bar walls were full of pictures of old Crediton. It seemed the current landlords had a love of growing things: plants filled corners and hung down in baskets from the middle of windows. The place had an earthy smell about it.

Not long after they had found a table, two men entered. Rosa was immediately aware of their minor Compulsive Talents. She turned to draw Narsin's attention to them, but he was already looking their way. A woman came out from the kitchen and placed food on the couple's table next to them. Rosa waited for her to turn and beckoned her toward them.

She was strong in the Talent, and she eyed the two men at the bar warily. In her mid-twenties, she was tall and willowy. Her hair had been dyed a deep shade of green, which matched the sparkling green of her eyes. She was dressed in black denims and a white top long enough to be tied with a sash at the waist.

When asked what they wanted, Rosa ordered two leaf salads, a glass of Spanish Tempranillo for Narsin and a small tonic water for herself. They could see that the woman was feeling uncomfortable under the constant gaze of the two men. Rosa also felt uneasy, so they took their time eating, as they wanted to see how things would play out.

Rosa could feel the growing anxiety of the waitress. After the men left, Rosa and Narsin talked and agreed that they would stay in Crediton until they knew the woman was safe.

They returned to the pub that evening and, after their meal, crossed the road to a place where they had a clear view of the pub's entrances and exits.

Near closing time, a car pulled into the square. It was growing dark. Rosa could only just make out the two men sat in the front seats, but her Talent told her they were the Compulsives. Narsin and Rosa moved back into the shadows.

The pub's patrons started to drift out at eleven and, after a period of noisy chatter, the square slowly became deserted and silent. It was nearly midnight when the woman emerged from her shift into the empty street. She looked around warily and headed towards a car parked half way across the square.

Narsin and Rosa were hidden in the shadows. The two men got out of their car and began to move towards her. The woman saw them and, struggling to find the car key in her bag, she panicked and dropped it. The men started running in a desperate attempt to reach her before she could get into her car. Judging the situation, Rosa acted.

The woman looked in horror as the ground opened up in front of the men then swallowed their feet. Their momentum sent them flying forwards and the woman heard the sound of bones breaking. She watched terrified as Narsin crossed the road to the screaming men. Speaking softly, he told them, "If you harm her, we will come for you." He nodded to Rosa and she released them, making them scream even more.

The woman stood transfixed at the scene before her. Rosa spoke quietly. "You need our help. Here is our number." She thrust a card into the woman's bag.

Saying nothing, the woman jumped into her car, started her engine and sped out of the square.

Chapter 2

The woman's name was Tara. She had been raised in Bristol, but had left to study in Oxford. She had a degree and a Masters in Anthropology and was obviously over-qualified for her current job.

Her story was complex. She had worked closely with the archaeologists who had discovered an important new hut circle on Dartmoor. It was an isolated spot below a large granite tor, and the team of two male and three female archaeologists had gained permission to camp there during the excavation.

Tara had been recruited to try and piece together the lifestyles of the people who had lived beneath the tor. She was to do this from the made objects they had left behind. The objects were unusually highly decorated for the period. The team found jewellery, ceramics and even some bronze weapons. Markings etched into the pots showed women working together and men skinning animals. There was a wealth of material here, and Tara loved doing field work.

It felt good working in a team. Everyone was so enthusiastic and, although she was an outsider in academic terms, they all took her very seriously. After the artefacts were cleaned, she carefully photographed each piece. She would work mostly from these photos and her notes and only ask to see the originals again if she needed to.

All seemed to be going well until one of the team brought her a bracelet. It didn't fit the period of the layer they were excavating. It was bronze, but the design was almost Celtic. Abstract, but with idealised trees woven in between the pattern. It was quite beautiful.

That night the team sat around the campfire and discussed it over a few bottles of Tribute Pale Ale and a plain meal of baked beans and egg. Dartmoor can appear a forbidding place, but the team sat joking and laughing, and the world felt fine. Tara asked if she could keep the bracelet for a while. She explained that she might be able to find matching patterns on the Internet. Something was nagging at the back of her mind. She had seen this pattern before, but where? She only had a few weeks left before she returned via Bristol to Oxford, and she wanted to do as much as she could before then.

Back in her tent, she surfed the 'net looking for matches. The nearest was from a find in central Spain, and that too had been unidentified. She wanted to know what it would have looked like to the wearer, so she placed it on her wrist.

~

When they found her the next day, she seemed to be asleep. Her fingers were bloodied and her hair tangled. She had pulled away the undergrowth from a cave beneath the rocky tor that overshadowed them. She was lying inside unconscious.

When Tara woke up, she found herself on her camp bed. Karl, one of the team, was sat next to her.

"You OK?"

"I guess so. Why are you here?"

"You don't remember anything?"

Tara suddenly sat upright.

"A cave, yes. Oh, it's no good; I can't remember much. I just felt I had to go in there."

"Why, for heaven's sake? Everyone's gone to take a look and it's just rock. Nobody understands why you were up so late scrabbling to get into it."

Tara was tired and couldn't be bothered thinking about it any more. Ignoring Karl, she lay back on her pillow and slept.

~

Everyone seemed to have forgotten the bracelet. The following morning, Tara tried to take it off, but she couldn't get it over her hand. Benign in all other ways, she slowly began to take it for granted. Several weeks later, she left on the planned visit to her parents; she had fond memories of her childhood in Bristol.

Her parents were Anglo Catholic and attended the Church of Saint Augustus in Westbury on Trym. Tara, whose faith had long since left her, went only to please her parents. She agreed to go with them on the Sunday, thinking she might bump into some old childhood friends. The church was just as she remembered: Gothic and rather gloomy. As soon as she entered, she felt the bracelet tightening around her wrist. She looked around, feeling everyone was watching her, and fought to stay calm, but her parents felt her discomfort.

At home, they asked what was wrong. Outside the church, the bracelet had eased and she felt comfortable again. Brushing off their concerns, she assured them all was well, but she knew it wasn't. Since returning to Bristol, she had felt increasingly uneasy. She liked being with her parents, but felt she needed to return to Oxford to write up her notes.

~

On the train journey back to her college, she had settled into a window seat and was casually watching the countryside when she suddenly felt uncomfortable. A man in his late forties, smartly dressed and accompanied by a tall, thin lad came and sat opposite her.

The two appeared very different. The older man was slim. He was dressed in a tweed suit with a small white flower in the buttonhole of his jacket lapel. His shoes were highly polished, and on his nose rested a pair of half-glasses. He appeared every bit the country gentleman. The tall, thin lad next to him was very different; dressed in a scruffy tracksuit with a hood, he seemed sullen and bored. The older man addressed her.

"Are you travelling far today, my dear?"

She had taken an instant dislike to him, but somehow felt compelled to answer. She told him she had been visiting her parents. Her destination was Oxford, the place where she worked. The more questions he asked the more she found the ability to resist answering them. He seemed annoyed at this.

When the train got to Reading, they all disembarked and she headed for the connecting train to Oxford. She would not see him again until much later. It was after this encounter that her life began to change. She began to feel more and more uncomfortable.

Her status as a research associate allowed her rooms in the college. Previously, she had felt proud of her achievements and enjoyed her life there. Now it was being overshadowed by feelings of unease. She had seen the lad in the tracksuit a few times. He was obviously following her, and not very good at hiding it.

One night, while walking home from dinner with friends, the bracelet suddenly tightened around her wrist. She looked back and saw the lad talking to two men. She began to run and did not stop until she got to her rooms. Throwing some clothes into a bag, she left to go to her car. When she arrived in the car park, the three of them were waiting next to it. Her fear left her and she became angry.

"Get away from my car," she shouted.

The men in suits just smiled and began to walk towards her. She held her ground, and the bracelet tightened around her wrist. Some instinct made her call on it. Suddenly, she could smell the roots and leaves of ancient trees. She pushed the men aside with the power that surged through her, got into her car and fled.

There was a couple she knew who would help her. She just needed to get away. They had been living in a converted double-decker bus while restoring an old cottage in the village of Bishop Morstead, north of Dartmoor. Those who rushed through life and never got out of their cars would call Morstead 'just a gear change on the road of life'. They were, and are, sadly mistaken.

Tara was not the sort to go to festivals. Most of her life had seen her head bent over books. A friend convinced her that the festival scene was a good place to chill and meet interesting people. She took some convincing, but finally gave in. It was there she had met Jess and Harry. They were very different from the people she knew in academia. There the people had a tendency to be competitive and shared as little of their research as they could. Jess and Harry seemed to thrive on the opposite. They were caring and open and always listened with curious ears to anything one had to say.

She rang Jess when she knew she was in trouble, asking - almost pleading - for a place to stay. Jess just laughed and told her to come at once. Jess and Harry had gutted the cottage and spent all their spare time turning it into the home they had long dreamt of.

It was a labour of love and, before it was fully finished, Jess insisted they move in. The old bus was empty now, and Jess told Tara she could stay as long as she wished. She had been living in it for six months before the men had located her.

After her encounter outside the Three Hogs, she knew she could stay there no longer. Now she was desperate. She emptied her bag onto the van table and looked for the card that Rosa had given her.

Chapter 3

Rosa and Narsin had only driven as far as South Molton when the phone rang. Narsin picked it up and answered. A rush of words came out of the phone.

"Please, please: I need your help. I need to talk to you. Please, can you help me?"

"Put only what you need in your car and leave straight away. They cannot follow you now, but if they knew where you worked they probably know where you live. Drive straight to South Molton and meet us in the car park behind the Pannier Market. My name is Narsin and the woman with me is Rosa Meldrum. We will answer all your questions, then you must make some decisions. We will help all we can."

Tara felt reassured. She packed a bag of clothes, then put them with her laptop and her precious notes into her car. There were no lights showing in the cottage, so she left a note saying goodbye. She started the car and drove off towards South Molton.

When she drove into the bottom of the car park, it was very late. She passed the cattle pens of the livestock market and pulled the car over. Lights flashed from a car at the top. She began to worry. Had she made a mistake? She bent forward with her head in her hands, shaking and afraid.

After fifteen minutes, there was a tap on the passenger door window. It opened and the woman from outside the Three Hogs sat in beside her. She did not say anything, just left time for Tara to come to herself. After a while, Tara turned to her.

"Can you tell me what's happening?"

"Not yet," was Rosa's short reply. "First, I must know who you are and what has happened to draw you to their attention."

"I don't understand; who are they?"

"Your name first."

"Sorry; I am Tara Carter, and you must be Rosa."

"Listen, Tara. I want you to come with us to our farm on Exmoor. We can explain everything to you there. Do not be afraid; we have only your best interests at heart. I want you to let my partner Narsin come with you in your car and you to follow me in mine."

"What will happen if I don't come with you?"

"They will not give up. There will be no safe place for you. If you come with us, we will develop what is within you and you will have no need to fear them. We will not keep you against your will. If you come and then decide to leave, there will be consequences, though none that will bring you harm from us."

Tara stayed quiet for a while and Rosa said nothing. Narsin was standing outside the car now. Tara's mind was racing. She knew what she had done to the men in Oxford; she had seen what Rosa had done to them in Crediton. Rosa was in control. She showed no fear. There was no one else she knew who could help her.

"What do you gain from all this?"

"Nothing, other than what you want to give."

Tara nodded, and Rosa slipped out of the car. Narsin replaced her.

"Rosa will drive down towards us. Start the car and follow her. We are going to a remote place on the moor. Don't be afraid. We'll explain everything tomorrow."

Narsin was not a great one for small talk, but he recognised the need for it now. He told Tara stories of his growing years and the wildlife of the moor. Tara began to relax. Surely a man that loved nature so much could wish her no harm.

It was three in the morning when they finally reached the farm and Rosa and Narsin's cottage.

Chapter 4

The next morning, Tara awoke to silence. It was long past the dawn chorus and everyone had gone to their work. Rosa had shown Tara around the cottage when they arrived, but she'd been too tired to take anything in.

She remembered the cars being parked in an old barn, then having to walk through the dark until they reached some buildings. Rosa had led her to a room in a quaint old cottage set back into the hill, and shown her into a bedroom. Rosa told her they would not be far away; if she needed anything she was to call. Tara had no idea what the time was, and when she looked for her mobile phone she could not find it. Maybe she'd left it in the car.

She would get herself washed and dressed before she went to find them. Grabbing her wash bag, and wearing her old dressing gown, she went in search of the bathroom.

Dressed now, and fairly calm, Tara decided to go and look for Rosa. She went to the head of the stairs and suddenly felt a moment of panic. She stood for a while to settle herself, and then went down. When she reached the staircase half-wind, she could see an old woman sat near the window. She was dressed entirely in white and had close-cropped silver hair. A book was in her lap, but she was not reading. Her head rested on her chin and Tara guessed her to be sleeping. Not knowing quite what to do, she headed across to the door.

"Off somewhere?"

She turned to see an old man, also dressed in white. The old lady in the chair stirred.

"Awake at last, are you? Oh, look at you; another of my life's years gone. I am Meldrum and this old man is Konia. We are here to help you."

"I don't understand. Where are Narsin and Rosa?"

"Well, dear girl, they have their duties; you will meet them again at mid-meal – I think you call it lunch. In the meantime, we have brought you some bread and honey, and Rosa has given me one of her precious tea bags in case you take tea. Would you like some?" Tara nodded, and Konia disappeared into the kitchen.

"Now, Tara, I am going to tell you the story of Rosa. How she first came to us and what happened afterwards. Ask any questions you wish. After mid-meal, it will be your turn to tell us your story."

Tara listened carefully and did not interrupt.

When Meldrum finished, Tara asked her, "Why have you chosen to tell me Rosa's story?"

"Because, dear child, you are very much like her."

Tara did not resent being called a child by Meldrum; she could see she was of a great age.

"I cannot see how I am like Rosa. She was called by a spirit and chose to come. I haven't been chosen by anyone, just chased here by evil men."

"Two things: the men who chased you here were not evil, but misguided. They are under the control of a spirit you might want to call evil, but it too deserves pity rather than anger. It has an addiction that would kill us all, a need that cannot be controlled. It feeds on human grief and does all it can to cause it. We are tasked with stopping it from interfering in the human world, stopping it from causing the grief it feeds on. We are on the side of the

~ 15 ~

land's spirits, who would suffer with us all if he becomes too powerful. He has been defeated by us once, so is cautious, but he will fight on as he has no choice, and neither do we.

"The second thing is: you, just like Rosa, are called by a spirit. You bear her mark on your wrist. The bracelet you wear is of Durantia, the spirit who walks between the dryads and their trees.

"Now come, I must eat. Old people get a bit grouchy if they don't get fed regularly. After mid-meal you can tell us your story, then maybe I can help you come to know yourself and the spirit that's chosen you."

~

Tara was surprised by the amount of people gathered. They were sitting around the long table that stretched the length of the meal room. She was seated between two young men at the end nearest the door. Meldrum and Konia joined Rosa and Narsin at the head of the table. Rosa stood.

"We welcome Tara to the House of Meldrum. Tara, will you say the grace of your faith?"

Tara was taken by surprise and hesitated before standing and repeating the grace that was spoken at the mealtimes of her youth. Rosa nodded to Narsin and he spoke the grace of the Pixsan.

"Spirits of earth and river; Gaia, mother of us all – we give thanks for what has been laid before us."

Tara identified with the sentiment of Narsin's words. She decided she would ask him about it when the opportunity arose.

Over the course of the meal of simple salads, the young man next to her tried to engage her in conversation, but her head was so full she could not respond and just nodded when she thought it was appropriate. When the meal was over, Meldrum and Konia came to her.

"You may have noticed that we no longer have the step of youth in our feet. Like our Spanish cousins, it is our custom to sleep for an hour after mid-meal. Feel free to wander the farm and go back to the cottage in an hour or so."

Tara promised she would but, before she had taken ten steps away from the meal room, a young girl appeared at her side. "Hello, I am Cormorita; you can call me Orita – everyone does. I am your guide and, if you wish it, your sister-friend."

"Okay, Orita; what exactly are you guiding me to?"

Orita stopped and turned to look Tara straight in the eye. With a slight edge to her voice, she told Tara, "You are not of us, but you have been called. You have no idea of our ways; you must learn them if you are to survive. Your Talent has opened within you. Meldrum will teach you how to control it so that you do no harm to yourself or to those whom you love. It is a hard discipline to learn. I am here to teach you the ways of the Pixsan. The Tort Mae have tasked me with this and when you meet them they will ask you if you will accept me as your sister-friend. I'm much younger than you, but my knowledge of this family is great."

"Do you do this willingly?"

"Yes, I love the history and lore of my people."

"Then, we will be friends, for my work has always been about discovering the lore of others. I must tell you that I am anxious and unnerved at the moment; a sister-friend seems to be something I need."

"Good, the Tort Mae have learnt from the coming of Rosa and Charly. Luckily, a young girl called Cormi befriended them and made their passage to our culture easier. You will come to know that we have students here, but they are all Pixsan. Only Wilds like you need people like me. You know that Rosa shares your heritage and she now leads us. I will start to show you around the farm today. I'm proud to say we are organic and almost self-sufficient. Tomorrow, when you are not with Meldrum, I will begin to teach you the Histories."

~

When Tara returned to the cottage, she found Meldrum and Konia waiting for her. Meldrum questioned her about her past: her upbringing as a one-spirit worshipper, her studies and her recent experiences. Meldrum nodded to Konia when Tara told of her lost time in the cave.

"It seems you have been chosen, and now you have some hard decisions to make. If you leave here, you will either be captured by the agents of our enemy, whom you know to be of malintent, or you will successfully hide from them, but at the cost of your mental health.

"Few like you survive unless they are trained to use their Talent. The worst case scenario is that you will be sectioned and treated with strong drugs. This nearly happened to another of the Wilds who now lives with us. I suggest you seek out Josie and ask her about her experiences.

"You have a career which is going to be hard to give up; this you must do if you are to avoid the fates I have lain before you.

"Do not be disheartened: your life is about to become more interesting than you could ever have thought it to be. Talk to Rosa and Narsin and Josie and Anna. I am sure Orita will do her best to instruct you in our ways. Now your training must begin. Sit and focus your mind on the bracelet you wear on your wrist."

Chapter 5

Later that day, Rosa sat with Konia in his study. "We've no idea where the men who followed Tara came from, or who they were acting for, but this gentleman she described makes me worry. He may have money and power, and if he has been seduced by Cernounos it could be very dangerous for us all."

"Before the girl arrived, we were making progress tracing the events that may have been the result of Cernounos' intervention. From studying the local news, it appears that there has been quite a lot of trouble between the old families on the council estates south of the city. It seems that fights start between the young and spread to the adults. Sooner or later tragedy will occur. It was just the sort of thing Cernounos did amongst the ancient tribes of the Celts. Could we send Josie and Anna to see what's happening on the ground?"

"They are the obvious candidates, but it will leave us short at the Skill Centre."

"I think it is time you asked the Tort Mae to find you assistants or to let some of your trainees stay on to help the newcomers."

"You are right, Konia; we will have to call the Tort Mae anyway as they will need to know about Tara. Can you talk to Josie and Anna and give them all the information you have?"

~

Anna hated driving their old VW on the motorway and insisted they make the journey by driving via Minehead and the A38. This would bring them directly into south Bristol and avoid the dreaded M5. The VW was slow, and they always ended up with a convoy of cars behind them. The summer was at an end now, so visiting families had returned home. Only the walkers remained: the sturdy oldsters who came wearing expensive walking boots and carrying alpine walking sticks.

They stopped in Minehead for fuel, then followed the coast road as far as they could before turning inland towards Bridgewater. Josie had read as much as she could about the council estates on the southern edge of Bristol. They had begun to be built in the 1950s. There were a few high-rise blocks, but most of the estates consisted of houses and maisonettes. There was a lot of bad housing in Bristol at the time. Areas labelled as slums were subject to compulsory purchase orders and demolished. Whether they liked it or not, the inhabitants were moved out to the southern estates.

Most of them welcomed their new, clean and heated dwellings, but many resented being moved from their communities to areas so far from the city centre. Despite this, new communities soon became established, and families intermarried and grew stronger.

Just recently, things began to fall apart. Josie and Anna were on their way to find out why. They were headed to an estate called Withycliffe. It stood at the foot of a high ridge that overlooked the city and from its summit you could see as far as the Brecon Beacons in Wales. Many of the houses backed directly on to the fields of the hill. Cernounos could make contact here. They needed to find out if he had.

A pitch for the van had been booked for them. It was on a small campsite below the Dundry slopes on the edge of the estate. Anna wanted to tell the site owners that they were sisters. Josie was having none of it.

"We are not putting up with any more of that shit; they can take us as they find us. It's their fucking problem, not ours."

Anna didn't think it was quite that easy, but gave in without argument.

When they arrived, the owner, a tall guy with a thick black beard and shaved head, didn't seem to care where they parked. He appeared more interested in the cigarette he was rolling than them. The site had a small shower and toilet block. Anna parked as near as she could. They were the only van on that side of the campsite. A fence closed in what Josie thought was a place for permanent residents.

It wasn't late, but they felt too tired to go out exploring, so Josie opened a can of baked beans and made some toast to put them on. Anna opened a bottle of mead wine. The two were well known at the House of Meldrum for their cluelessness when it came to the culinary arts. They loved good food, especially Corrin's, but not enough to learn how to cook it. After reading for a while, they finally gave into the tiredness they both felt and snuggled in under the duvet.

Chapter 6

The flimsy curtains were useless against the bright autumnal sunlight that shone through the van windows the next morning. Anna was the first to stir. She looked down lovingly at the sleeping Josie and put the kettle onto the stove. Josie, awoken by the smell of freshly brewed coffee, sat up in the narrow bed.

"I don't know what we are going to find today, but I can't say I'm that positive about it."

"Let's see; it may be nothing, but if we find anyone, I don't think you will be in any danger, not with me at your back."

Josie laughed. "No, not with you at my back."

They left the van in the campsite and walked into the estate. It was bright, with a slight autumnal chill to the air. The windows in the high-rise blocks glistened in the sunlight. As they walked further into the estate, they could see lots of contrasts. Big, well-kept gardens next to overgrown ones. Some of the houses were well maintained; others desperately needed a lick of paint.

The main shopping area looked rather sad. There were a few shops open: a greengrocer, butcher and a Co-op minimarket. The bank was closed and its windows covered with steel shutters. No clothes or shoe shops. There was a queue for the post office, which was at the back of a small general store.

Josie and Anna headed for the edge of the estate where the Dundry slopes met the back of the houses. They walked along a back lane with garages on their left and a copse on their right. As they walked, the lane veered away from the estate and deeper into the trees. Josie and Anna stopped and looked at one another. They had sensed something up ahead.

Just beyond the next bend, they could see a tall lad in the distance. His face was covered with the hood of his jacket. He seemed to be talking to someone in the trees. He suddenly turned towards them, then quickly back towards the woods. Josie knew immediately that he was a creature of Cernounos. She signalled for them to turn and leave.

They had stumbled on something they had feared finding: a servant of Cernounos talking with his master. There was nothing they could do, so they would just report back. They explored a bit more of the estate before returning to the van.

Having booked, Josie decided they would stay for the night before heading into Bristol to see the priest. They had just finished eating when they heard a noise outside. Someone was trying to open the door. Anna drew back the curtains and saw a figure moving away. The tall lad and three others stood fifteen feet from the van. Anna turned to Josie.

"Are you ready? I am going out to face them."

"Be careful. I don't know how strong the boy is and I don't want him to see where what hits him comes from."

Anna stepped out to confront them.

"Hello, little vandal boys; what can I do for you?"

"Get the bitch. We need to take her to him!"

Anna laughed contemptuously. Filled with anger, the tall lad ran towards her, only to hit a wall of air. The others hung back.

"So, he is right: his enemies have come."

"Yes, we have come and we will keep coming. Your master will cause you nothing but grief, but we will not let him bring grief to others."

With this, Josie started up the van and Anna jumped in. They sped past the lads, who made a feeble attempt to run after them.

Chapter 7

Josie and Anna drove towards Bristol, where they pulled into a lay-by on Bedminster Down.

There were a couple of other free-camping vans there. The police never bothered them unless they stayed for more than a few nights. Tomorrow they would visit the priest. For now, they would try to ignore the wind that had begun howling outside, and try to get some sleep.

In the morning, they pulled out of the lay-by just as a police car pulled in at the other end. Josie breathed a sigh of relief. Her background would certainly have come up on the handheld computers the police carried. Best to avoid complications.

Josie and Anna had mixed feelings about going back to the city. It was where they had spent their formative years. Years that had not always been happy ones.

They drove right into the middle of the city, to a district which bordered its major shopping centre. History had seen this district go from a rich Georgian suburb to a place of inner city deprivation. Now it was home to a vibrant West Indian community.

There was still danger here. The city centre attracted people with all sorts of problems. This was the reason Gary had chosen it. In collaboration with the Pixsan, he had set up an inner city Refuge. The Tort Mae considered that Wilds might drift there, and supported it generously. It had been purpose-built with the advice of security and psychiatric experts.

Gary cared little for this and kept the doors open throughout the daylight hours. He was a priest convinced by holy vision. He cared only for his mission to protect the vulnerable. Occasionally, he had the help of the local Pixsan, but only if they felt there was a Wild amongst his clients they could do something for.

~

Josie and Anna arrived late in the afternoon. The Refuge was in an old square. At one end was a church whose architect must have been confused about which style to follow and ended up with a mish-mash of many. The Refuge itself was in a modern building at the other end of the square.

The door was open and, inside, the Day Watch sat with a friendly dog.

Josie and Anna walked in and were about to announce who they were when the Day Watch spoke up. "I know you two; you've been before."

He asked them to wait. They walked into the reception room but, before they could sit, they were confronted by a young man. He had risen from his seat as soon as they had arrived in the room. He spoke to them in a language they recognised but did not understand.

Anna took a cool look at him. Jesus, she thought, if I fancied men I would definitely fancy this one. He was of average height, confident and totally relaxed. He was not rugged like Narsin nor did he have the charisma of Corrin. He had a boyish look. He was dressed in a multi-coloured shirt and harem trousers that were well worn and torn at the knee. Beside him was a backpack complete with bedroll and sleeping bag.

He smiled from a face surrounded by jet black hair and through a mouth enclosed by a flimsy yet attractive beard. He tried another language. Josie looked at him blankly, so he tried again.

"Señoritas," he began, but now Gary was in the room and the two women were on their feet.

Gary hugged them both and made to lead them out of the reception room. The young man coughed and Gary turned. He spoke to the man in broken French and the young man nodded. Turning to the women, Gary announced. "Josie, Anna: this is Rafael. As far as I can make out, he is from a remote region bordering Galicia and Portugal. He asks if I know of the Trasnos here. He says he can feel this is a place where they come and go and is sure I know of them. I have explained that I do not."

At this point, the young man stepped forward and held out his hand to Anna. She ignored him, but Josie, bold as ever, clasped it in her own. She laughed and he stepped back, looking a little embarrassed.

"He is one of us, Gary, though his Talent is weak and I am not sure what it is he seeks."

"Can you please take him with you when you go? He has been here every day for weeks asking the same questions."

"We will ring Rosa later. Narsin can speak to him in Pixsan and find out why he's here. Let him come with us. He is harmless and he won't understand a word we say anyway."

After checking in with all the staff, Gary led them to the lift that would take them up to his private quarters. A code was needed for the lift to rise beyond the second floor to the penthouse where Gary lived. The three-bedroom apartment could only be accessed by the lift and exited by a fire escape that lowered, New York style, to the fire stairs below. The Tort Mae valued his safety and those they would send to stay with him, so they had insisted on this arrangement.

Josie and Anna told him of their encounter in Withycliffe and wanted to know if he had seen an increase in Wilds arriving at the Refuge. He told them there were more people coming, but he did not know how many had Talent. He needed a Pixsan present to help. Perhaps the new trainees could come to help the Wilds as part of their training. Josie was not sure about this, but would put his request to Rosa and the Tort Mae.

That night, after Rafael had finished speaking with Narsin, he handed the phone to Josie, who spoke with Rosa about Gary's request. She also asked about Narsin's conversation with Rafael, but Rosa said she could not say what had passed between them as Rafael had pleaded confidentiality. Rosa would not tell them what she knew, but they guessed she knew everything. No secrets existed between Pixsan partners.

Rosa had agreed that there was a need for a Pixsan to be permanently based at the Refuge and said she would call a meeting of the Tort Mae to request it.

Having established Rafael was Pixsan, Gary agreed he could stay with them for the night. The following day, they left for Devon, knowing only too well they would have to return soon to confront the situation in Withycliffe.

Chapter 8

Rafael stood alone and nervous at the door of the Place Apart. He had been called by the Tort Mae. He did not question this because he knew it would not help him to do so. His name was called and he entered, bowing deeply to the woman in green who stood at the far end of the room.

Speaking in Pixsan, she asked, "Do you accept the authority of the Tort Mae?"

"Yes."

"We welcome all Pixsan here, but you come unannounced at a time of conflict with the spirit, Cernounos. Tell us why you have come."

"Because you have those amongst you who can see. You will know that I am weak in the Talent, yet I was called by our river spirit. She told me I must travel here to seek a woman, one whom I must serve without question. I know it is common for us to travel to find life partners, but our people have not left the place you call Iberia for many generations. I am at a loss to know why I am here, although I know this is where I am supposed to be."

"What are your skills, Rafael?"

"In my home community, I am one who grows and nurtures plants. I have studied the science of it remotely and practised it on our lands. My main interest is arboriculture. For many years we have acquired forest land to stop the march of commercial Eucalyptus trees into our hills. As for me, well, I grow and manage fruit trees."

"We cannot help you in your quest, Rafael, but we recognise your need and will allow you to stay, as long as you work each day as your skill allows. You may look to Narsin as your mentor. When he has time, he will guide you in the ways of the House of Meldrum. Go and find those working in the field; they will know how best to use your talent."

When Rafael had left the Place Apart, Rosa was called, and she placed before the Tort Mae the case for a Pixsan at the City Refuge. The Tort Mae considered this and suggested that those fresh out of training lacked the experience needed. It was agreed that Ariana was the person who had all the skills required. She had been trained by Meldrum in the ability to remove Talent and she had always held the talent to manipulate memories. Ariana would be recalled from the House of Malarta in Spain and a suitable replacement would be sent.

~

Rafael did not take long to find the person he needed. The farm had a walled garden where the soft fruit and vegetables were grown. In Galicia, he had orchards for fruit trees to grow in. Here, in this limited space, they were grown as pruned cordons on south-facing walls. Genuinely fascinated, he listened and understood all Anjea had to say, even though the Pixsan she spoke was accented in a way unfamiliar to him.

Other workers came when they noticed the newcomer, but Anjea sent them back to their work.

"There will be time to talk after family-meal. Let him have some space to get to know me before you paint me as a tyrant in his imagination. He may never be able to shake those images off."

The others laughed and shouted, "Watch out for her: many a young man has failed to do so and missed their destiny."

"Shut up, you fools," she shouted. "Do not listen to them; they are trying to discomfort you. Even in such a small community as ours there are those who constantly goad out of jealousy, vanity, or just plain wilfulness. Their first-born child will settle them; bright green eyes are very powerful."

From experience in his own community, Rafael knew all this to be true and was used to it. He did not care; their behaviour was not his problem. These were Pixsan people and in a few days he would grow to know them and they to know him. This did not concern him, but the words 'absolute obedience', which kept circling his mind, concerned him very much.

Chapter 9

Tara was getting used to the Pixsan. Everybody took their work seriously, but they seemed to be laughing all the time. They spoke a language alien to Tara, but always spoke to her in English, with pronounced West Country accents. She understood more as Orita carefully explained the Histories to her, though she still hadn't made up her mind about her way forward. Logic told her that she had no choice, but she still agonised over the fact that she would be abandoning the academic career she had worked so hard for.

After mid-meal, Orita failed to appear. Instead two women walked unannounced into her room. Tara thought she would never get used to the lack of doors and personal space, something the Pixsan didn't seem to notice.

"You must be Tara. Orita asked us to pop by."

Tara looked up at them. One had short black hair cut in a tight bob and the other had completely unruly red hair reaching way down over her shoulders. Neither were dressed in the white of the Pixsan. The black-haired one was dressed in punk-like clothes, tight jeans torn at the knee and a leather jacket badly worn at the elbows.

For some reason, the red-haired woman seemed to trigger the colour green in Tara's head. She could not have been more different. She was dressed in a floral top with a bright yellow, short skirt. On her legs she wore thick, bright red tights and on her feet powder blue boots. The black-haired one spoke first.

"I am Josie; it seems we share the same heritage. We are of the few non-Pixsan who bear Talent. Meldrum tells me you have some hard decisions to make. Let me tell you our story."

Tara sat and listened without interrupting, then asked, "You had no option but to stay – would you have felt differently if you had my background and future?"

"Listen carefully, Tara," said Anna, "if you leave here you have no future. If Rosa had not come with Narsin, then I would have lost Josie forever. To those in the world beyond the Pixsan, different is dangerous. You will not be able to hide what you are forever, and the only escape is no escape, just a life without Talent."

"Thank you."

"Do not thank us. The Pixsan allowed us to find ourselves: it is them you must thank."

Meldrum arrived just after they left.

"We have some difficult business, you and I. You need to stay and we need to know if it is safe for you to stay. This is what I ask: I need to enter your dreams and in return you can enter mine. We will both be vulnerable when we do this, but we both need to know how strong you are."

Tara did not answer straight away. Meldrum waited. The seconds ticked slowly by and Anna's words kept going round in her head. "There is no escape, just a life without Talent."

"What if I chose to give up my Talent; could you take it away?"

"I could, but I would not. I am not sure how your spirit would react. You bear her symbol, but it is also a talisman from which strength can be drawn. You might want me to take your Talent, but your very being might instinctively resist and with what you can draw on I might no longer be here. I have not long been reunited with the most important person in my life. I want a few more years yet."

"Is there anybody strong enough?"

"No, and your Talent may be linked to your intellectual ability; if you did find a way to lose it, you might end up with mental illness."

"You give me no options."

"Believe me, Tara, if there were options I could give you I would. You are young and in conflict. You love your studies, but they are just dry interpretations of something long past. Look closely around you: you are living in a community that has survived those long years. You could become Pixsan and share their heritage. You have magic within you and I can help you to live it. Like many others, you can believe in the magic of the past, but fail to see the magic in the present. Open your eyes, Tara, for beyond the blinkers there is another world you could be part of."

Tara thought of her parents: their deep belief in a saviour that would rescue them from a corrupt world. She began to realise that no saviour she could envisage would be coming. Now she must learn her part in the fight against the destruction of the natural world. She would become Pixsan.

Chapter 10

Rafael was right about the community: once they recognised that he really did have a way with plants, he was soon accepted. Narsin had taken an interest in him and in the land from which he came. Rafael created pictures in words of the thickly wooded mountainous area of Galicia where he had spent his childhood. He'd lived there happily until the spirit had called him.

Rafael admitted he had a little English, but claimed he was too embarrassed to use it. Narsin explained that he had a little Spanish, but that he too was a little embarrassed to speak it. Rafael offered to teach him in exchange for lessons in English. Narsin explained he was far too busy; however, there were a few youngsters keen to visit the House of Malarta who'd been studying Spanish. Maybe they would help.

Rafael agreed, though he felt a little awkward when two fifteen-year-old girls arrived at his rooms over the wood store. They took their learning and teaching very seriously, and he soon gained confidence in his use of English. The girls were very studious and asked lots of questions. On several occasions he had to admit that he was not sure how to answer; he explained that Spanish was his third language after Pixsan and Galician.

Pixsan white replaced the colourful clothes he wore when he arrived. He felt a desperate need to fit in and not be noticed. He carried out his work quietly and kept to himself. He took books from the small library next to the meal room and retreated to his own rooms as soon as family-meal was over. He was here, where the woman he must obey would eventually find him, but he was not going to make it easy for her.

Chapter 11

Itana stood in the square outside the meal room. This place was so Pixsan, but so unlike anything she knew. When she looked up, all she could see were the hills that surrounded the farm. The trees had lost their leaves as the season of Autumn was near its end, but everything to her eyes was overwhelmingly green. Itana was named after the mountains near her home. Summers there were hot and dry, winters were cold and grey.

This was her first time away from the House of Malarta and she was not really sure why she was here. She had not intended to travel. Her work with the families' horses was a joy to her. Then Cormi came. Cormi who sang with the Tanners and who had come to tour with a group of Pixsan musicians from all over Iberia. Cormi had a wonderfully disarming way of awakening people to possibilities they'd not thought of.

When Cormi returned to the House of Malarta from touring Eastern Europe, she had been feted by all, for she was instrumental in bringing the lost sister home. Her voice alongside the voice of the Daughter Tessa was perhaps the most well known amongst her generation. Itana was in awe of her, despite the fact that she was just a few years older than herself. Cormi had awoken something in her – curiosity, a need for adventure – she still didn't know.

When Cormi arrived back from the tour, it was late and she was exhausted. She had been assigned a bed in Itana's rooms. This was normal. Personal space matters little to the Pixsan. When Itana awoke, she saw Cormi sat on the edge of her bed, looking at her.

"I feel I should know you."

"Oh no! I am a distant cousin of Leana. People say we look alike, but I don't see it."

"You are right. Anyone with true sight would know."

"Who do you think you are, Itana?"

"I am what you see."

"Really? Have you no life inside your head that sees things differently?"

When she was endlessly brushing down the horses, Itana knew that she would like something different, but she did not know what.

"There is something about you. I will talk to you later. I need to settle back here in the House of Malarta first."

And now, far away in the hills of Devon, Itana questioned herself. Why was she so unsettled? This was something she had wanted. She was here in the House of Meldrum with Cormi as a roommate. It would help if she knew why Cormi was so keen for her to come but, until she knew, she was determined she was going to make the best of it.

She entered the meal room where all were gathered for family-meal, and sat at the foot of the table. To her right was a girl with dyed green hair and to her left a boy with the long ponytail of a Pixsan male and an amusingly sketchy, boyish beard. She guessed that they were newcomers to the House as this was where newcomers and honoured guests alike were seated.

At the far end of the table sat the two legendary Daughters, Rosa and Josie. Rosa stood.

"We welcome Cormi back to the house of her birth, and her friend Itana. Itana, will you honour us with the grace of your family?"

Itana said grace in her native Valencian. Rafael was surprised and, as soon as Itana sat, he could not stop himself from thanking her in Galician, a language with similar roots. Itana smiled, then, turning to the woman next to her, asked where she might be from.

Tara's schoolgirl Spanish soon established that English would be the best way for them to communicate. Despite their different backgrounds, the two women soon found things in common. Rafael was rather relieved; he was quite happy to be ignored. As soon as possible he got up and left. He did not get far. The two women ambushed him just outside the door up to his rooms. Itana stepped forward.

"Well, Galician boy, you seem to be quite a mystery. My friend here says you hide away up there in your loft as if you were frightened of the world. Maybe it's just us women you're scared of."

He ignored them, opened his door, and hurried upstairs. He could hear their laughter. He shook his head in anger. Until some new students arrived, he was going to be stuck at the foot of the table with them for every meal.

"That was cruel," Tara said. "He is obviously very shy."

"Sorry, Tara," said a laughing Itana, "there is no such thing as a shy Pixsan male. There is a mystery there and I am going to get it out of him. Thanks for telling me about him. He might not like me at first, but I am sure we will

~ 40 ~

all become friends in the end. It will give me something to do while I try and work out why I'm here."

Chapter 12

Withycliffe was a problem that had been discussed with the Tort Mae, and it was decided that Rosa and Narsin would go with Josie and Anna to see what could be done. Rosa thought it best to deal with it straight away, so they were now travelling up to Bristol in the old VW van. They had decided they would tackle the lads head on, just drive into the main square and wait for the news of their arrival to spread.

Josie was up front driving and Anna was listening to music through a set of headphones. Rosa took the opportunity to talk about the new arrivals. Turning to Narsin, she asked about Rafael.

"He works hard and keeps his head down. I think he has a dread of the woman he has been sent to find. He is certainly avoiding everyone in the evenings and I think the only female he engages with is Anjea. They both have a deep interest in their work. Anjea has declared, so I think he feels comfortable around her. What about Cormi's friend?"

"I have asked Cormi why she brought her here and she is not really sure. Cormi wants her to meet Charly and the others at the House of the Mer. She admits she might be mistaken, in which case Itana will return home, taking only new experiences with her."

"And Tara, what do you think?"

"Meldrum tells me she is very strong in the Talent and thinks she has a key role to play in the struggle against Cernounos. There is no doubt the spirits are gathering forces for a final solution and I think all the

Daughters will be part of it. Tara has her own spirit in Durantia, but when the time comes I think she should come with us to the Ictath water. At the moment she is still unsure and a little unstable. Itana seems to have adopted her; I think under her and Orita's wing she will lose her doubts and see that her future is with us. She is keen to finish the project for her department in Oxford; there is no reason she cannot do that from the farm. I will talk to her again when we get back."

~

It was late afternoon when they arrived in Withycliffe. They had parked up on double yellow lines in the main square near the library. No traffic enforcement officer would be around at that time of day, and they wanted to make themselves as visible as possible. Word would soon spread.

Josie and Anna left the van and sat on a bench facing the boarded-up bank. Only the convenience store was open, and that was on the far side of the square beyond the library. Rosa and Narsin stayed in the van. It was not long before a group of youngsters entered the square. A young girl left the group and approached the sitting women.

"What do you want here? You don't belong here; best clear off."

A young lad joined her. "Best do as she says, unless you want trouble."

Anna looked up.

"We are not interested in you," she said dismissively. Then, turning towards a group of lads walking into the square, she said, "It's them we're interested in."

The girl followed her gaze and, with a warning look at the others, indicated they best leave.

Josie and Anna remained sitting as the lads approached. The one they had recognised as an agent of Cernounos was leading them. His hood was back this time. They could see he had dark brown hair and a handsome face, a face which belied the anger festering behind it. He had a long coat resting over his shoulder, with the arms hanging loose at the sides. The other lads hung back, a little deferential, waiting for him to make a move.

"You're going to come with me this time, and you are not going to make a fuss. He lifted a sawn-off shotgun from beneath his coat."

Josie looked up, appearing totally unruffled by the gun-wielding lad. They stood as if ready to obey him, then Anna said, "Did you not hear me last time we were here? Your master will cause you nothing but grief. Now, be sensible and put the gun away."

He lifted the gun higher.

"Get moving or I will take you to him dead. It matters little to him, or me."

The lad sounded serious, but Josie and Anna still did not move.

He moved the gun higher and, as he did, the paving slab beneath his feet tilted, making him fall forwards. Pushing the barrel to one side, Josie tried to pull the gun from him. He resisted, so she called on the wind and pushed him down. The gun flew from his hands and slid across the pavement. One of the other boys moved forward to pick it up, then suddenly stopped. He stood, staring blankly at his leader who was knelt sobbing on the pavement.

Anna walked over to him. Looking down, she spoke quietly. "Your gift has been taken from you. Your master will not want you now; you are no longer of use to him." She looked at the other boys. "Learn from this!"

Josie and Anna walked slowly back to the van, carrying the gun. Josie jumped in the driver's seat and Anna sat silently beside her. In the back of the van, a tearful Rosa was being hugged by Narsin.

Taking someone's Talent away was hard, even when it was the boy's simple compulsive one. Every Talent bearer feared the loss of their Talent. Taking it from someone else, no matter how corrupted, took its toll on the taker. Narsin held on to her tightly as they left Withycliffe to take news of the Tort Mae's decision to the priest.

~

When they arrived at the Refuge, it was dark and the doors were locked. Josie parked the van on the pavement in front of the entrance and Narsin jumped out. He pressed the buzzer and, after a few seconds, Gary's voice came from the speaker. He told them that the Refuge was closed for the night and was just about to tell them where they might find shelter when Narsin spoke the word Pixsan into the microphone. The door immediately buzzed open and they could hear footsteps rushing down from one of the upstairs meeting rooms.

"You should have told me you were coming."

Josie was obviously amused.

"And you were going somewhere, Father?"

"OK, point taken. Look, I've got to finish the session I'm holding upstairs. I won't be long. I will ask Sarah to come and make you some drinks."

They were about to object, but Gary was already on his way up the stairs. A few minutes passed and a small blonde-haired woman came down. Anna looked up, surprised.

"Good grief; it's Auntie Sarah!" Josie looked at her quizzically. The woman rushed across the room and embraced Anna.

"What on earth are you doing here?"

"Long story. Let me introduce you to my partner Josie and my friends Narsin and Rosa."

Sarah just nodded at Narsin and Rosa, but stared intently at Josie.

"You are the girl she fell in love with at the college where we worked? She was too frightened to ask you out, and then you ended up in that dreadful hospital."

"Oh dear, Josie, said Anna, now she will tell you and the others how much I fretted. Seriously, in that awful time Sarah kept me sane. She was like an aunt to me, hence her name."

Josie smiled as she walked across to where Sarah stood.

"Well, Auntie, tell me everything. You must know she is a wilful woman and I need every advantage I can get."

At this, all four women burst into laughter. Narsin just shook his head.

When Gary came back, Josie and Anna told him they were going to stay the night with Sarah and her partner Clare in their house in St Werburgh's. They would come

~ 46 ~

and pick up Narsin and Rosa in the morning. Narsin and Rosa waited until Gary had finished his rounds, then they all said goodnight to the Night Watch and went up in the lift to Gary's apartment to bring him up to date.

The day's events in Withycliffe worried him, but he was pleased that Ariana would be joining him at the Refuge. He had not met her, though knew of her and how strong she was. He thought that God must know how tired he felt.

~

After their return to the farm, Rosa met up with Meldrum and Konia to discuss the events in Withycliffe. Konia was noticing a pattern developing on the outskirts of the city. It seemed that wherever it met the countryside, Cernounos was trying to gain a foothold. Konia had suspicions that all this was just a distraction, that there was something bigger going on, something that was linked to whoever it was that had tried to abduct Tara. Nevertheless, they felt that everything had to be investigated, and this meant that Josie and Anna would be frequent visitors to the City.

Chapter 13

True to her word, Itana never let up with Rafael. Each night after family-meal she made sure Tara and herself were ready to leave when he was. He rarely spoke to them and never answered their questions as they walked with him to the woodshed. He hoped his silence would drive them away. Itana thought otherwise. Tara became a bit unnerved by Itana's insistence they walk with him every night. He obviously did not want their company.

She tried to convince Itana that they should leave him alone, but Itana insisted that he needed to open up, and she was going to help him. Cormi had watched all this happening and was amused at first, but eventually felt sorry for Rafael. That evening, when the women left the meal room looking for him, they were surprised to see Cormi call to Rafael and walk off arm in arm with him towards his rooms.

Itana turned to Tara.

"Well. who'd have though it? Cormi and that boy!"

"Jealous, Itana?"

"Certainly not!"

The strength of Itana's denial made Tara think that her statement was not entirely true. He was a handsome lad, she thought. It might be easy to fall for him.

It would be a while before they found out what they were desperate to know.

Cormi had sought out Rafael when he was working in the garden. She had learned some Valencian from Leana during her travels with Valencian musicians. She guessed it was similar to Galician and spoke to Rafael in Valencian first. He was surprised and curious. While he worked, they talked about her music and her time with the Tanners. Despite himself, he found Cormi's company a relief.

"Now, Rafael, I know Itana has been giving you a hard time, so let's cause a scandal. I will be waiting for you after family-meal tonight, and when they come out they will see us walking arm in arm to your rooms." He laughed, thinking it would be good to get one over on Itana, but he had reservations. Surely Cormi could not be the woman he was sent to find. She was the singer of the lost sister song. She could not be the one. With these thoughts, he agreed.

When they arrived at the door to his rooms, she insisted on being invited in.

"I can feel they have followed us, so we must keep up this fiction. When I know they have given up, I can use the trap door down into the woodshed and go out the back way. Unlike me, they were not brought up here, so will not be aware of another way out."

Cormi explained that as a small girl she often came to the woodshed. The rooms were just storage space then. She loved the smell of newly cut wood and liked to rummage through the old storage boxes to see what she could find. This was all before Narsin gained permission to convert the loft into rooms.

She settled in one of the chairs near the front windows where she could be seen from the lane and took the glass of mead wine that Rafael was offering. Cormi did not press him for the reason he was avoiding the girls. He felt at ease in her company.

Rafael described the mountains and forests of his home and Cormi talked of her travels in Eastern Europe. It was late when she left to go back to the room she shared with Itana. When she arrived, Itana was sleeping. She would not know what hour Cormi got back to their room.

Rafael had some wry looks when he turned up for work in the garden the next day, but nobody said anything. Itana was rather in awe of Cormi. There was no way she was going to ask what was going on. Tara was quietly relieved, as she was beginning to think that what started as jest was becoming a bit like harassment.

All this had been a distraction for Tara, now that Meldrum was making her work harder. Not only did she need to know how to anchor herself when using her Talent, she also needed to know about Durantia and the Dryads. Meldrum had said she would introduce her to the Guardian, but first she must do everything she could to prepare herself. Anchoring was something she must master above all else. Meldrum demanded that she spend her evenings in reading and research. She was still working on her paper for the Oxford project, but she would finish that soon. She was settled in her mind that she would not go back to Oxford and decided she would resign her post once the paper was submitted.

All this work meant that if Itana wanted to discover Rafael's secrets she would have to do it without Tara. Itana was keen to carry on, but each night Cormi had his arm before she could get to him. After a few tries, she gave up.

What had started as a lark for Rafael and Cormi had ended with friendship. Even after Itana had given up, Cormi often walked with Rafael to share a glass of mead wine in his rooms. She asked Rosa one day why Rafael had come and what she thought his antagonism with Itana and Tara was all about.

"Haven't you guessed, Cormi? Why do Pixsan men and women normally travel away from their families?"

"Ah, I see; he has come to find a life partner. Then why is he so antagonistic towards Itana and Tara? They are handsome and intelligent women and he could do worse."

"I think there is more to it than that. Narsin tells me that his river spirit was quite specific about how he must act towards the woman once he found her."

"Specific in what way?"

"I cannot say, Cormi. Rafael told Narsin and asked that he vouch for him, but not divulge any of the reasons for him being here. I think he was reluctant to leave his home and resents the task given him, but he is Pixsan and will complete it. In the meantime, he seems to be making life hard for himself. What do you think?"

"Oh, he is not so bad."

"Cormi?"

"No, no, I may have helped him avoid Itana, but he is not for me."

"How do you know this, Cormi?"

"He can't sing or play. He is nice enough and we are good friends, but that's all."

"If you say so, Cormi. In that case, don't let him get a crush on you."

Cormi looked thoughtful when she left to begin helping in the kitchen.

~

Tara still had a room at Narsin and Rosa's cottage, but she rarely saw them. They arose really early, completed their run, and left for first-meal before Tara was up and ready. Sometimes in the evenings, Josie and Anna would come. Tara was always invited to join them, but she felt a little awkward and spent most evenings with Itana. Now that Meldrum had taken up her evening time with more study, she had little time to relax. Today, Tara felt exhausted. She had been up early in an attempt to put the last touches to her report for Oxford, but before she had finished Meldrum had arrived.

"How are you feeling, Tara?"

Knowing that there was never a simple answer to a question set by Meldrum, she replied, "I am fine, and you?"

"Yes, yes, my dear. When is a Meldrum not fine? I want you to be well today because we are going to the woods. You must be at your best to achieve the next step of your training."

"In that case, I must be honest with you, Meldrum. I am tired, very tired. I have been trying to finish the Oxford paper and keep up with all the work you have been giving me."

"I see. Well, tomorrow or the next day will do. Finish the Oxford paper today and take a few days off. I need you fit and fully aware for the next stage of your training."

"Thank you, Meldrum. Let me finish this, and you will have my best attention."

Tara turned back to her work. Just a few more hours, she thought, and then she could put her old life behind her.

That evening, Cormi made a point of meeting Rafael on his way home. When they were back in his rooms, Rafael sensed some tension in the air. They were friends, so he did not hesitate before asking what was wrong.

"The problem is not with me, Rafael; it is with you. Tell me why you are doing your best to avoid all the single women on the farm?"

Rafael was silent.

"I am your friend and you should trust me. If you don't want to explain, that's fine; whatever it is, you will have to confront it in the end."

More silence.

"OK." Cormi got up ready to leave.

"No, wait, Cormi. I will explain."

Rafael told her of his encounter with the spirit of his community and explained that it was something he had not wanted. "Have you been in the presence of the Ictath, Cormi?"

"Yes, several times. I was told I was to go to Spain with the Daughter of Song to seek the Daughter of Fire."

"You did not resent being torn away from your community?"

"No, for me it was the beginning of a great adventure."

"What if the Ictath spirit had told you to travel abroad and seek a man whom you must serve unquestioningly and with absolute obedience?"

"And is this what you were told?"

~ 53 ~

"Yes, but it is not the Pixsan way. We take partners as equals. I will not submit to a life of servitude."

"And how do you think that avoiding Itana and Tara is going to help?"

Rafael did not answer.

"Did the spirit say that the woman you are to serve was to be your partner? Did she say that this would be for a lifetime? You know the spirits are not very clear when they talk of future paths. Rafael, you will not avoid whatever path awaits you by hiding away. Embrace it. Find out what it is you face and, when you know, you will know what to do. You too could be on the path to adventure."

More silence. Then: "You are right, Cormi. I have been a fool. I resented being torn away from my beloved home in the mountains to face a future of uncertainty. I see I must change."

"Good," said Cormi in a rather stern voice. "You can start by inviting Itana and Tara for mead wine after family-meal tonight."

Rafael was about to object, then thought better of it.

"Very well; I will ask them when we get there, but I think Meldrum has been making Tara work in the evenings, so I am not sure if she will come."

When they were all sitting for evening meal and the grace had been said, Rafael asked the two women if they would like to join him and Cormi for a glass of wine later. The two women quickly accepted. Itana could hardly eat her food after that. Her mind was racing. Why were they being invited? Were Cormi and Rafael about to declare? It was a bit soon. Were they to be the first to know? Tara, on the other hand, knew nothing about couples declaring and thought that all of them getting together was just a nice idea.

They walked back to the woodshed together. Cormi asked the women about their day but Rafael stayed silent. When they got to Rafael's rooms, Tara and Itana found seats near the window and Rafael was about to head for the kitchen when Cormi told him to sit and she would fetch the wine. Itana turned to Rafael.

"Well, thank you for the invite, but why are we here?"

Rafael did his best to look cool. "Why not? We are all new here; it is time we got to know one another."

"This is a change of heart, Rafael."

"Yes, that's right. I have had some problems to work through and Cormi has been kind enough to help me."

With this, Cormi re-entered the room with the wine. Itana was convinced there was something more to it than Rafael's simple explanation, but as the evening wore on she began to accept it. Tara was the one who eventually asked the question Rafael was dreading.

"Why have you come here, Rafael?"

He looked towards Cormi.

"I have been sent on a mission by our river spirit; however, the details of the mission were not made clear. I will know when events lead me to the path I must follow."

"It seems we have that in common: my spirit wanting me to be here, I mean – but, in truth, I was chased here by men who were trying to capture me for Cernounos."

Rafael looked shocked. Itana turned to Tara. You never told me everything; tell us the whole story.

Tara did tell them everything, and the telling of her story was to be the glue that held them together as friends.

The next day, Rafael got more than wry smiles in the garden. He ignored the comments and got on with his work.

CHAPTER 14

Ariana had been tempted to fly back from Spain. Her research into modern aircraft made her realise that they were mostly made of alloys. However, she could not cope with the idea of being so far away from the earth that grounded her. She travelled up through France and took the shortest ferry crossing. She could tolerate iron, but it was a discomfort she tried to avoid.

Josie and Anna met her at the ferry port and they headed straight for Bristol. They gave her all the news as they drove. Ariana was curious about Tara. Another potentially powerful Wild Talent.

Josie and Anna introduced Ariana to Gary as soon as they arrived.

Gary was really pleased to meet her at last. She was just as Rosa had described: quite tall, with jet black hair and skin as pale as ivory. She looked at Gary through bright green eyes, bowed from the waist, then extended her hand. Gary took it and, as he did, he felt something brush his mind.

Ariana smiled. "I am sorry for the intrusion, Gary. I felt you had something hidden from yourself in the back of your mind. Now I know what it is we can work on it while we are working together."

Gary looked at her, not knowing what to say. The casual way she had entered his mind without asking disturbed him. "You could have asked."

"Don't worry about it, Gary. Ariana has your best interests at heart. The Pixsan never intrude far without asking first."

Anna laughed. "Not if you're anything to go by, Josie."

"Ah, but I'm your partner, girl."

"We are off now," announced Josie. "We are going to stay with Aunty Sarah and Clare tonight, then head for a little recce in Kingsham before we go back."

"Josie, you could have stayed here."

"Sorry, Gary, we want to catch up with our friends."

Gary turned to face Ariana.

"Let me show you your quarters. I am afraid you will be staying in my suite. It is secure in this dangerous part of the city. There are three-bed sitting-rooms, all ensuite, with kitchenettes and a common room, so you should be comfortable."

He made to lead her towards the lift when she turned to him and said, "Why are you afraid, Gary?"

"It's just a turn of phrase, a form of apology."

Ariana was smiling, and Gary thought she was teasing him.

Ariana quickly settled into her work at the Refuge. Unlike Gary, she could spot the conflicted as soon as they came through the doors. Some she could only help by removing their Talent. She was one of the very few Pixsan who could.

Meldrum had felt she had this Talent and convinced her she needed to develop it in case anything happened to herself or Rosa. Ariana hated doing it, but knew this was the only way a life for the conflicted might be possible. Very few came who were not conflicted, but when they did she could help them come to terms with what they were.

From the Refuge, they would be sent to a Pixsan farm in a remote area of Wales. They would be held in a place apart until the Welsh Tort Mae decided what to do with them.

The majority who came had no Talent and were just troubled youngsters. They all loved Ariana. She was a great listener and took them all seriously, offering advice and support. She rarely mixed with the professionals who visited, always presenting herself as just another volunteer.

Ariana and Gary spent their evenings discussing the clients and exchanging stories. Ariana teased Gary relentlessly when he said something that could be interpreted in a way he had not intended. They were becoming good friends, and then it happened.

It was just another day, then suddenly four armed men forced their way into the Refuge. Gary had his back to the door of the reception room when they came bursting through. As he turned, one of the masked assailants fired his gun into the ceiling, shouting for them to be still and say nothing. They made Gary turn to face the wall and told him not to move or he would be shot. He waited quietly until he was sure he couldn't hear them. Then he slowly turned around. There was no sign of Ariana. He rushed into reception, where the day watch was still standing facing the wall. Gary called for him to turn around and asked what had happened.

It was all so quick. He had seen them carry Ariana out, shouting they would fire if she did anything stupid. They had put a black cloth bag over her head, and then he saw them bundle her into a large, black car outside.

Should he call the police? Gary told him not to and that he would deal with it. After settling the worried staff, he headed for the lift to his apartment and a phone call to Rosa Meldrum.

Shock went through the Pixsan community. Nothing like this had happened to them in centuries. They did not want the police involved; that would only complicate things. They felt powerless.

The Tort Mae were called to the farm. The strongest with Talent were gathered, but they did not know where to start. Josie felt that Ariana was being held by allies of the Trickster. Who else would be interested in her? He had been active between the farm and the south and east of the city. Konia and Meldrum had been monitoring the 'net for any signs of the unusual. They all knew that Ariana was one of their strongest and that whoever had taken her might have no idea how strong she was. She may escape without their help, but they would try their best to track her down.

Josie and Anna left for the Refuge that day. They needed to talk to Gary. When they arrived, they found him distraught. They had never seen him like this. He was pacing around the apartment and could not stay still.

"I blame myself. The security here is useless against determined gunmen."

"Stop that now! You are no more to blame than any of us. Let's go through this. Is there CCTV?"

"Yes, but they were masked. We have photos of the car number plates, though we have no way of tracking them."

"Gary, you have no way, but you do not have Konia and Meldrum. Send them a picture of the car. Now let us talk about what has been happening in the weeks running up to this. Anything unusual? People hanging around you don't know? New entrants?"

"I am not sure, but Ariana felt something. Ever since she'd arrived she thought there had been a Talent hanging around outside. We thought he was a client waiting for the moment to come in, but now I don't know."

Josie was worried.

"The Pixsan have become complacent whilst our enemy has become bold. It seems clear you were being watched by a Talent sensitive who felt Ariana's presence and reported back to our enemies' agents. Now they've got her, what are they going to do with her? Something is odd here. I think Cernounos is afraid of us and is unwilling to tell his allies too much. He might be letting them feel their way. Ariana has many skills, but she has no protection from the knife or the gun. Her Talents are not like mine and Rosa's. If it is a Wild who has her, she may yet have a chance."

Josie phoned on one of the old pay-as-you-go mobiles the Pixsan used. Rosa wanted them to stay and see what else they could find out. Konia and Meldrum had been working on the plates and monitoring the media. She told them Gary might need their help. If the takers returned, they needed Pixsan who could deal with them physically. Josie reluctantly agreed, but knew that Rosa was right. They moved their things from the van up into Gary's apartment.

Chapter 15

Ariana did not struggle or cry out. She just sank into a much-practised calmness. It would be pointless for her to fight back. Her captors had weapons which she had no defence against. She needed to find out who they were and what they wanted. She could cause confusion by taking away their memories, but she couldn't do this to all four of them at once, and it would make the situation more dangerous. She knew one of them was trying to use compulsive Talent on her. She would do as he said and play along for now. They stopped just outside of the city and made her sit upright.

Two of the men left the car and, a few moments later, she heard another car starting up and moving off. She could hear the driver turning in his seat to look back at her.

"The man beside you has a gun. Do not think of doing anything that might cause him to use it."

She felt something prick her arm and the next thing she knew she was waking up in a small room.

She sat up on the bed and looked around. The room was obviously partially below ground, as the narrow oblong windows were at the top of the walls. A smell of lavender hung in the air. There were bookshelves, pictures, and little homely touches that made it seem less like the prison it actually was. Across from the bed, a door led into a small ensuite. She assumed that her captives were agents of Cernounos. In her usual state of calm, she sat and waited.

Two men in suits came for her at about 11 o'clock. She could tell they were trying to use Compulsion on her. She did what they asked. They walked along a corridor and past a room where two guys sat playing chess. One was a tall black man and the other white. Both their Talents appeared small. They looked up from their game and glanced across at her. She was wearing loose-fitting chino-style trousers and a baggy jumper, but even in these unflattering clothes she was undoubtedly attractive. The men turned back to their game.

She was led out and up the side of the house. She looked around at the large formal gardens. It seemed that she was being held captive in the basement of a large country residence. They entered the house through French doors at the end of a wide terrace which overlooked the tree-lined driveway. There was a tall, thin man waiting for them. He was dressed in an English county style, wearing a tweed suit and waistcoat, highly polished brown shoes and even a flower in the buttonhole of his suit collar. He spoke with an upper-class accent.

"I must apologise for the way you were brought here, my dear, but I doubt you would have come voluntarily, and I do need to talk to you. I believe your name to be Ariana. Mine is Gregory. My man in the city tells me you hold a powerful Talent, but he himself is insufficiently Talented to say what that might be. Now, Ariana, what exactly are you?"

Ariana remained silent. She could wipe their memories one by one and leave them in a state of confusion, but she decided she wanted to learn as much as she could before taking any action. Their use of armed gunmen was worrying. Only a few Pixsan could fight back against such weapons.

"I am Ariana, a woman."

"Yes, Ariana, but what we want to know is what extra qualities you have? My men here have a certain way of convincing people."

"Guns do tend to be very convincing, Gregory."

"You might find just how much if you keep toying with me."

"I don't think so, for shooting a woman would go against everything you believe in."

"So you think you can read people. I wonder, is that your Talent?"

"You could say that."

"Then tell me about David here."

"What exactly do you want to know?"

"His character, his special ability, anything you think relevant."

She looked at the man for a few minutes. He was shorter and slightly scruffier than the other one. His suit jacket was a little too big and his tie too loose around his neck.

"He is good at talking people into things. He is loyal as long as his salary is being paid."

"And Colin?"

She looked across at him. Smartly dressed with highly polished shoes, an immaculately clean white shirt, and a suit that fitted him perfectly. "He is good at talking people into things as well, but he is fiercely loyal to you. He sees a future at your side. For him it is not about the money."

"Very good, Ariana, and you can perform this trick at a distance?"

"No, only if I am in the same room."

Colin and Dave escorted Ariana back to the basement, but not to her room. Dave pushed her through the door and locked it. Ariana found herself in the room at the end of the corridor with the two men. They looked at her appraisingly. Minor Compulsive Talents, she thought, and sat down at the table with them.

She introduced herself and got their names. The tall black guy's name was Rex. The shorter white guy was called Nick.

"So, one leaves and another one arrives. What do they want from you, Ariana?"

"Good question, Rex, and one I have been asking myself. Why would they send four armed gunmen to kidnap a volunteer worker in a refuge?"

Nick looked impressed.

"Four armed gunmen to kidnap one woman. They must think you are pretty special."

"Well, we all like to think we're special, but not that special. Now, tell me about yourselves."

Nick opened up straight away, telling her enough for her to guess that he was being held in an attempt to trace a more powerful ex-girlfriend. She was not sure about Rex, but she guessed it must be something similar.

So they were prisoners here, she surmised, because Cernounos had been manipulating the man upstairs. Gregory must be really wealthy to live in a place like this. She asked the others who they thought he was. Nick said that when he was interviewed by him he thought he recognised him from the television. A politician maybe. Ariana suddenly put it all together.

He must be the right-wing MP Gregory Clarant. Ariana took little interest in politics but news of him winning a by-election for his party, Britain First, was big news. It even headlined in Spain, where the rise of populism across Europe was viewed with alarm.

She got up to go to her room. Halfway there, she stopped and turned, saying, "Oh boys, I think I know why Clarant sent four armed men to get me: he thinks I must be dangerous. Just between us, I can tell you he's right. I am dangerous – very, very, dangerous!"

Chapter 16

Tara was rather puzzled by Rafael. He had sidestepped her question. She still had no idea why he was there and reasoned it was none of her business, so she didn't give it any more thought.

They began to meet regularly after family-meal. Tara was becoming more convinced than ever that Itana had set her cap at Rafael, but he didn't seem to notice. All four had become good friends.

Cormi was spending more time working on her songs and was often absent from the gatherings at Rafael's rooms. She was soon to move to Torrington where The Tanners were recording a new CD featuring Cormi and some of the musicians she had discovered on her travels in Eastern Europe.

Tara's training had progressed well. She had learnt how to use her Talent without harming herself or others. Her focus was improving. The next stage was to learn everything she could about the spirit which had called her. Meldrum wanted her to begin studying in the evenings again. She agreed, but managed to convince Meldrum that every other evening should be enough as she would need time to digest what she had learned. Meldrum suspected that she would spend her free time in the company of her friends, but cared little as long as she stuck to her studies.

The Monday that Cormi was due to leave, Tara received a letter from Oxford via her parents and the complicated forwarding arrangements the Pixsan used.

Her work had been praised by the archaeology team, and the university department expressed much regret at her resignation. They assured her that should she wish to return in the future an application for any post would be considered favourably.

Cormi said her goodbyes after mid-meal. Later that evening, Tara and Itana met with Rafael. When Tara told them she would only be free every other night, Rafael immediately suggested they only meet up when Tara could join them. Tara sensed Itana's disappointment. She began to think that Rafael was not so unobservant after all.

The following day, Meldrum wanted them to walk together in the old woods. Tara could only just keep up with Meldrum who seemed, at times, to have the energy of someone much younger. The woods stretched across the leeside of one of the hills which surrounded the farm. The main part was largely unmanaged, with only a small part being coppiced. The very centre of the wood was full of tall ash and beech trees competing for the light. Near the edge of the woods, oaks predominated, and it was here that Meldrum led Tara on their walk.

The whole woodland had an enchanted feel about it. Tara reached out to the trees around her and felt calm and uplifted. Suddenly, both turned their heads to the edge of the woodland. They were being called to the lone oak by the Guardian of the woods. Meldrum turned and walked ahead of Tara until they had left the trees and could clearly see the Guardian Oak on the side of the hill. They sat beneath its branches.

Nothing seemed to be happening, but just as she thought she was falling into a deep sleep, a voice entered Tara's head.

"Welcome at last, you who are Durantia's chosen."

Tara felt the presence of the Dryad. She knew she was not dreaming as she walked beside a young Pixsan girl towards the edge of an escarpment. They looked down over endless woodland."

"You have come from the Familiar world into the Strange. You are the first of your kind to do so for many years. We will teach you how to walk here. We know you have been given the secret of anchoring your spirit to your body. Soon you must discover the one who will watch over you in the Familiar, while you travel here. For now, come and sit by me; we will help you understand more of the paths that lay before you."

Tara awoke to find Meldrum beside her, gently snoring and fast in her sleep. She did not disturb her, just sat thinking of the place from which she had just returned. The majesty of the trees and the multitude of their colours. Maybe the earth was like this once and maybe it should be again.

Chapter 17

Tara needed to pick up a book from Konia that evening, so she was late arriving at Rafael's door. Just as she was about to enter she was confronted by an angry Itana coming down the stairs.

"Itana, what's the matter?"

"Ask the stubborn pig upstairs. He keeps telling me his mission is more important than anything else. Oh, Tara, I think I've made a terrible fool of myself."

"Lets go back to your room. Cormi's gone now so we can talk."

"Do you have any mead wine, Tara?"

"I have a bottle or two; we'll pick them up on the way."

Rafael was not surprised when Tara did not make it past his front door. What a bloody mess, he thought. Thank you, Cormi, he cursed, but he knew she had meant well.

Their gatherings took a while to recover from that evening. Tara missed Rafael's company, but felt that she would somehow be betraying Itana if she went to see him.

Tara threw herself into her studies and Rafael returned to his old routine. Mercifully for Itana, she no longer had to sit at the foot of the table next to him. New students had arrived, so the group of friends had been seated separately among the family. Rafael was rather relieved to find that a new student had been assigned the spare room in the woodshed. A strong, square-built, tall Pixsan from the Yorkshire moors named Denfar. Not many knew that he was one of the few Pixsan males gifted with a major Talent. It was to be a while before Rafael discovered just what his Talent was. In the meantime, they found they had a shared interest in herbal plants, and soon became friends.

Rafael and Tara never avoided one another and, at one point, he tried to explain things from his point of view. He said he had done nothing to encourage Itana and Tara knew this to be true. Incredibly, the strong, independent Itana had set herself up for a fall. He asked Tara to come one evening and meet Denfar and to bring Itana. Surely, they could put the past behind them. Tara asked Itana and, to her surprise, she agreed.

"I'm over it, and I can't go on avoiding him forever."

Tara breathed a sigh of relief. This was the Itana she knew.

After family-meal, they walked to the woodshed together and met up with Rafael on the way.

"Denfar will be joining us later; he is still with Narsin and Meldrum the Elder."

"What exactly is he studying?" asked Itana.

"I am not really sure, but he shares my interest in plants used medicinally and rumour has it that he spends hours with Meldrum the Elder when she is not training Tara."

They headed upstairs to the rooms over the woodshed and settled down with their glasses of mead wine. The atmosphere was a bit tense for a while until Tara told of her encounter with the Dryad. Then they were all full of questions. Rafael stressed how jealous he was of her ability to communicate with the spirits of the trees.

They were all laughing at some joke Itana had made when Denfar appeared in the doorway. Suddenly, Itana went very quiet. Tara turned to see a very tall, stocky man with a ponytail of black hair. His deep green eyes surveyed the room and finally settled on Itana. She had shrunk back into her chair with a look like fear on her face.

"I see you have come, Itana. I thought it might be you."

The mood had changed from jovial to strange in seconds.

"I am sorry, but I think Itana and I need to talk." He turned to her, asking, "Shall we walk?" They left, leaving Rafael and Tara looking at each other completely bemused.

"What just happened?"

"I have no idea, Tara."

"Why did Itana look so afraid?"

"I am struggling, like you. Denfar is a nice enough guy. I like him, though I would hardly have thought him and Itana a match. Maybe I am looking at this in the wrong way. Perhaps there is something they have to do together. I'm sure we will find out."

~

They continued to meet up in the rooms above the woodshed. The days were becoming lighter and warmer, so the log fire was no longer lit. It was fairly symbolic anyway, as heat to the farm buildings was supplied from a heat well near the old shed where Rosa kept her car. Unlike most of the buildings, the woodshed did not have the insulation benefits of thick cob walls, so the woodfire added a sense of warmth to the room, making it feel cosy.

In the evening gatherings, Itana and Denfar always sat apart from one another. Denfar listened attentively when Itana talked of her home and her work with horses. She seemed to be back to her old self, confident and, to Rafael's thinking, a little opinionated.

Tara could not work out what was happening between them. Rumour had it that Itana was now attending Denfar's training session with Meldrum and Narsin. Denfar had never confided in Rafael about his reasons for being at the farm, and this suited Rafael as he was reluctant to talk about his own reasons. Their shared interests seemed enough to cement their friendship.

Tara, on the other hand, had no such reservations. After a few weeks of reigning in her curiosity, the dam eventually broke. Tara met Itana in her room just before they were due to walk to the woodshed.

"OK, Itana, what is going on with you and Denfar?"

"Itana burst into laughter. Tears were rolling down her cheeks as she folded her arms around her middle, trying to hold back more laughter."

Attempting not to show her annoyance, Tara asked, "Well, what was so funny?"

"The whole thing; that's what's so funny. Tell me what you think of Denfar."

"I'm not sure what you mean. He seems like a really nice guy."

"He is, but what do you see when you look at him?"

"I see a man who is well built, some might say stocky, big and tall, but not fat and with lots of muscle. He is broad in the shoulder. He carries himself upright and has penetrating eyes. I have seen him smile, but never heard him laugh. When he talks to you he is interested in what you say in return. Unlike Rafael, he actually listens. He always has his big cloth shoulder bag with him and favours a hooded cloak over a coat."

"Well, you have been looking! Do you fancy him?"

"Perhaps," Tara said, smiling to show she was not serious. "Now, tell me what this is all about."

"Not now, Tara. Let's go and meet them. I'll tell you soon, when I know more. The evening passed pleasantly, with Itana sitting as far away from Denfar as she could.

Tara was interested in the community that Denfar came from. He described its isolation and some of the hardness they endured during the long winters. He talked of his childhood, telling tales of adventure and folly.

Tara noticed that Itana was staring at him intently, following every word.

The next day, Rosa asked if Tara would move out of the cottage. They needed Denfar to move in, so that Narsin could act as his mentor. She could either move in with Rafael or Itana or move up to the skill school where there were a few rooms currently vacant. Tara did not want to move in with Itana until she knew what was going on with Denfar. On the other hand, the thought of taking the spare room at the woodshed did not appeal to her either.

On balance, she thought that the woodshed would be the better option. Rafael was out in the garden from dawn to family-meal, and most evenings they were all at the woodshed anyway. Rafael had shown no interest in her, so she knew he would keep to his own space. Itana was capable of playing all sorts of games and Tara did not want that at the moment. She had her own training to think about.

Rafael was non-committal when she told him she was moving in. He could hardly object, but she felt that he did not really care either way. Itana thought it highly amusing. Tara braced herself for the comments that were bound to come.

Chapter 18

Ariana's continued absence was worrying the Daughters and the Tort Mae. If she could have escaped, they should have heard from her by now. This worried Narsin, but he was beginning to think there was another possibility. What if Ariana had chosen to stay with her captors to find out more about them? They considered this, but decided that either way they had to try and contact her.

Meldrum talked to Tara about it on their way to the woods the following day.

"I wonder if the Dryads would help?" she asked.

"I don't know if they can. I'm not sure how they see us. Maybe we all have a different pattern they identify us by. I've never really thought about it. In any case, they would not have had contact with Ariana so will not know her. If I get the chance, I'll ask. Everything is worth a try."

Tara sat beneath the Oak that day, but the Dryad did not call, not that day nor in the days to follow. It was not until a few weeks later that she heard the call, and much was to happen before then.

~

Tara settled into the routine at the woodshed. Rafael was up and gone before Tara woke up. Her study time was split between training with Meldrum and studying from books in Konia's vast library. He was always on hand to help her. This left her with some free time and she enjoyed walking around the farm talking to the family and the students from the training rooms. Tara was learning so much about Pixsan life and philosophy and now thought Meldrum had been right, for she had swapped the dry study of the almost unknowable past for living within a part of it, a part which had survived and adapted over the centuries, but still kept its secrets.

Tara was heading home after one of these walks when Rafael fell in beside her. They talked affably of their day. Just as they rounded the corner, they heard calls for help.

When they arrived, they could see a man clinging to the ridge high up on the thatch of the building opposite the woodshed. The wooden hook on his roof ladder had given way and he was clinging on to the thatch itself.

"Get help," he shouted. "I cannot hold on for much longer." Tara did not move but reached out towards the woods. The smell of earth and trees filled her nostrils. She reached up to the man and held him pinned to the thatch. "Get help, Rafael."

When Rafael returned with Denfar and Narsin, Tara was still holding the man with the energy she was drawing from the surrounding trees. Her brow was covered in sweat and she was breathing hard.

"Hurry, I can't hold him for much longer." She reached out again and a new source of energy entered her.

Narsin grabbed the ladder to the verge and reset it; Denfar put his foot to the bottom while Narsin climbed. When Narsin reached the verge, Tara let the man descend in a controlled slide until Narsin could reach out and help him onto the ladder. When she was sure he was safe, Tara released him.

She was dizzy and would have fallen to the ground if Rafael had not caught her and held her steady. Staring at her, he spoke quietly so the others could not hear.

"It's you; you're the reason I'm here. You drew something from me to save that man."

Tara tried to answer. Rafael called out to Denfar, who had been looking at the man's hands. They had been cut and bruised in his desperate attempt to cling on. He walked over and examined Tara.

"All's well; she has just fainted. Carry her back to your rooms. I will call in with Itana later."

Rafael walked off with Tara in his arms.

Narsin turned to the unfortunate workman. "Resne, what have we discussed about unnecessary risk?"

"I'm sorry, Narsin. I thought it would be safe. I'll make sure there are two of us and all the equipment is secure in the future."

When Tara woke up she found Rafael staring down at her. He looked away quickly and asked how she was.

"I am well. How are you?"

"Tired. Whatever happened out there seems to have drained energy from us both. I will make some tea for you. It seems to revive you."

"Have some yourself, Rafael."

"No, no, I am happy with water."

When Rafael brought her the tea, she sipped it, and in the quiet that followed tried to fit it all together.

"What do you think happened out there, Tara?"

"I have only ever drawn on the trees once before, and that was when I was attacked in Oxford. I did it instinctively, not knowing how I managed to do it.

Meldrum has been helping me to do it in a controlled way. Today we were far from the woods and I was losing the link, so instinctively drew on the nearest well of energy, which turned out to be you. I am sorry, Rafael."

"Don't be sorry, for a life was saved. My question now is: what does this mean for us? I was sent here by the spirit of my people. She told me I must find the woman that I was to obey without question. I think that woman might be you, Tara."

Just then, Itana and Denfar entered.

Itana winked at Tara.

"Is he looking after you properly?"

Rafael stood up from where he was knelt at the side of the bed.

"I think some mead wine is in order."

As nobody objected, Rafael headed towards the kitchen to fill some glasses. Tara stirred herself and they went to the living area. Denfar took a seat by the window and Itana, as usual, sat as far away from him as she could.

"Well, my dear, it seems you are quite the heroine."

It was then they heard a noise on the stairs. They were all surprised when Narsin and Rosa entered the room.

"Thank you for saving Resne, Tara. The family owes you a debt of gratitude."

Tara made to say something, but Rosa indicated she be silent.

"Tara, you know Narsin and I are life partners, but what you don't know is that Narsin is my amplifier. This happens only rarely. It has happened in the distant past, but there have been no reports of this happening for many years. Not, that is, until the Daughters were called together to banish Cernounos.

Anna is Josie's amplifier and Dylan is my sister Tessa's. Narsin knew when Tara supplemented her own Talent with Rafael's that he was to be her amplifier. This is also true for Denfar and Itana. Denfar is not only a healer but, just as the healers of old, he has a minor Talent to draw on fire and air. Not as strong as the Daughters Josie and Leana, yet enough to make him the most powerful healer for generations. He can only realise his full Talent with the help of Itana, and you, Tara, can only do so with the help of Rafael.

It has been easy for Narsin and me because we are declared; you must find your own ways. Rafael, come and talk to Narsin if you need to know more or have doubts or concerns, but from now on you must leave your work in the garden and go each day with Tara to train with Meldrum. You cannot ignore this, or escape it. If you try, sickness will be the only result."

Nobody said anything and Rosa and Narsin got up to leave. Narsin turned to face them from the head of the stairwell.

"There is little doubt: you have been called together at this time to help in the continuing fight against Cernounos."

Chapter 19

Sir Gregory Clarant had never been a violent man, but now the game had changed and the stakes were higher. He was a man born to privilege – sent to Eton as a boy, then on to Oxford to graduate in Classics and History. When he left Oxford, he went straight to the finance quarter of the City of London. Here he proved to be a sharp dealer and within a few years amassed a large fortune of his own. Setting up offshore companies, and dealing right on the edge of legality made him extremely rich at a very young age.

When his father died, he was called back to the estate. His mother had no interest in running it and preferred to be in the family villa in the South of France. As the elder brother, Clarant inherited the estate; his younger brother inherited some properties in London. They had never been close, and he thought of young Jonathan as a hopeless hippy, always off on some crusade.

As far as Clarant was concerned, everyone could make it if they put their mind to it. If they did not, it was their fault, and they would get no help from him. His pet hate was what he called the Nanny State. As far as he was concerned, the state should have no role in helping the unfortunate. If they did not have the gumption to pull themselves up by their boot straps, then they must suffer for it. He was the founder of the new right-wing party, Britain First.

It seemed to him that there were many in society who shared his views. His new party had a racist undercurrent, which chimed with some, but Clarant did not care. They had voted for him overwhelmingly in a by-election; now he was the first and only Member of Parliament for Britain First.

He had been at Oxford when the almost forgotten researcher, Perry Beglott, had gained quite a following telling stories of the ancient spirits of Albion. Clarant had taken an interest but, before he could become too involved, Beglott seemed to have suffered a nervous breakdown and became reclusive. He published papers occasionally but, while they were informative, they were very dry and academic. Clarant had read them all with interest and sought out his earliest publications which were less dry and more enthusiastic. At that time, his main preoccupation had been the earth spirit, Cernounos.

Clarant would have forgotten all about it if he had not encountered the very spirit Beglott had been studying. It was his habit to walk the grounds of his estate before he took breakfast.

This particular morning, his curiosity was captured by a mist in the small copse near the brook. He walked closer, and in the mist he could just make out what looked like a tall man. Thinking it must be an intruder, he marched towards the wood to confront him but, as he approached, he felt the hairs on the back of his neck begin to tingle.

Clarant was a man who had never recognised fear, so he walked faster towards the figure. When he got close enough, he could see that it was a naked man, wearing nothing but a crown of leaves on his head. He tried to get closer, but his feet would not move. His efforts to call out produced no sound from his mouth. For the first time in his life he was afraid.

A powerful voice came into his head. Cernounos would help him: he would provide him with Talented servants. His wealth and influence would grow. Full of avarice, Clarant asked no questions. The visions that came to him were totally compelling. A man with so much greed could not resist them. What he was not told was that there would be a price to pay; by accepting Cernounos, he had become his servant. It was this encounter that had set him on his current path.

Knowing that some people had the power of Compulsive Persuasion fascinated Clarant. Cernounos had told him that some possessed even more impressive Talents. Clarant saw the possibilities in this for his own use and advancement. He had little Talent, apart from a very weak Compulsive one, and a strong resistance to those who did.

What he did have was money and power. Colin and David were his first recruits and were rewarded well. He also had four recruits in Bristol. One who could sense people with Talent, which is how he had discovered Tara, one with a Compulsive Talent and the two with minor Compulsive Talents who had fallen foul of Rosa in Crediton. He would use them to find the others Cernounos talked about, but would not lead him to.

Cernounos had been stripped of his power by the Pixsan and would have to move carefully if he was to grow again. He knew the Pixsan had the power to return him once again to a weak earth spirit, so he began his long game of using ordinary humans against them. He would have to be careful, for the Pixsan could hide easily among the Familiars.

He had one thing in common with the Pixsan: the spirit world must never be disclosed to the Familiars other than through the smallest channels. The Familiars must never discover why or how he was using them. Clarant would help him and his arrogance would allow him to think he was in control. He was, like many pawns, disposable.

Cernounos had judged Clarant's character well. He was obviously someone whose greed and lust for power could easily lead to the conflict and grief that Cernounos fed upon. He had led Colin and David to him. Now he was on his own. Cernounos would move on to make new recruits and distractions to keep Pixsan eyes from Clarant.

~

Ariana was sitting with Rex when they came for her. She judged Nick to be weak, but she liked Rex, and knew he wanted to escape. She would see how things developed, but thought he would be a useful ally.

Ariana was taken up to the room where she had met Clarant before. She remained quiet.

"Ariana, my dear," said Clarant.

Ariana visibly winced and turned to him.

"You want something?"

"Very direct, Ariana. Yes, we have some guests this weekend. I want you to tell me what you see."

"OK, that's it?"

"You agree?"

"It's not criminal to judge character. You think I can do it; I'll try."

"Nothing you want, Ariana? Surely you have some price in mind?"

"Gregory, there is always a price. Let's see what happens on the weekend. We can talk then."

"Nothing more to say, my dear Ariana?"

"No, I was in the middle of a game of chess with Rex. He is an interesting player. Can I return now?"

They took her back to where Rex sat next to the chessboard waiting to finish the game.

Rex stood and the suits looked at each other then left. Ariana paid them no attention.

"How the fuck do you do that – just bloody ignore them?"

"Rex, be still. We'll find our chance. I need you to trust me."

Rex looked at her. Shit, where did she find her calm?

"They will not let me walk in the grounds at the moment and I need someone who can. Can we work together? I will tell you what to look out for. Tell Nick nothing as yet."

"Nick, he is so wrapped up in himself I don't think he notices the sun coming up."

"We may need him, Rex, but not until the last moment."

"Last moment?"

"Rex, you'll know when that time comes."

"Nick walked towards them from his room down the corridor."

"Hey Ari, you're back. What did they want from you?"

"Who's Ari? My name is Ariana."

"OK. Well, what happened?"

"Just asked me for a favour. We'll talk about it when I'm ready."

~

Ariana had asked Rex to keep an eye out for anything unusual when they were out on their morning run, but he always reported back in the negative. Ariana pressed him to keep looking. Anything, anything at all, she kept telling him.

As the weekend approached, Ariana was called upstairs and offered a range of clothes to wear. Clarant told her it was a gathering of important people and she would be escorted at all times by Colin and David. She was not to approach anyone. Colin would tell her which people he wanted her to analyse.

Clarant need not have been concerned. Ariana had no intention of drawing attention to herself. There would be no one there who could help her. Only the Pixsan could do that, and she knew they would be working hard to locate her. When they did, she felt sure they would find a way to leave a sign in the grounds. She worried that Rex might miss it.

Early Saturday morning, she was collected from the basement by Colin. She had chosen to wear a plain white trouser suit which did nothing to flatter her figure. Clarant, who she felt was taking a little too much interest in her, had wanted her to wear a ridiculously figure-hugging dress, until she pointed out to him that she needed to go unnoticed to carry out her work. She told him that if she was approached she would say she was security, not a guest.

Clarant had talked about her with Colin. Colin was unsure.

"She seems to do everything we say without question, whether I use Compulsion or not. This worries me a little. I cannot really say what I think of her. She volunteers nothing about her background, other than that she has recently returned from working on a farm in Spain. I think she is like you, resistant in some way to our Talent."

"I see. We'll use her as long as she carries on cooperating. Keep a close eye on her. Have we heard from our Talent-seeker in Bristol yet?"

"No sir, not since a few days after we took Ariana. He may have been spotted and is lying low for a while."

"Let's hope so, Colin. I thought him a great asset. If we don't hear soon we will have to send the men back to find out exactly what is going on there."

The cars coming up the drive were all expensive, with some chauffeur-driven limousines among them. By midday, people were gathering on the terrace, talking and drinking. Most were couples, but there were some single men and women among them.

Ariana looked at the couple nearest her. The man was tall and close to being clinically obese. The woman was a few years younger, slim with blonde hair and sunglasses pushed back up over her head. Colin occasionally nodded towards someone and Ariana took note, reading as much as she could of their character.

Everyone there was dressed expensively and fashionably, but she was not interested in their clothes.

She indicated to Colin that they needed to move among the guests. One of the catering staff approached with a tray of drinks. Dave waved him away.

"Talk to me, Colin; we are beginning to look like a caricature of those stiff-backed plain-clothes security people who follow the Prime Minister about."

Colin turned to her and, for the first time, smiled.

"Please come this way, Ariana."

They wandered through the guests on the terrace, with Ariana making mental notes of what she saw. She had an almost photographic memory, so it would take little for her to recall the thoughts she had about these people. She spotted one of the single men walking towards them. Tall, blonde-haired and well muscled, she could almost smell his arrogance. He had a very minor Compulsive Talent. It seemed to her that he had always got his way. These types of Talent holders were totally unaware of their Talent; they just had a high opinion of themselves. As he moved closer, she whispered to Colin and Dave to hang back.

"Ah, a new face. Who do I have the pleasure of addressing?"

Ariana moved right in front of him and, putting maximum command in her voice, announced,

"Security, sir; please step back."

She raised an arm and beckoned Dave and Colin to her side.

"Your invitation, sir."

"My what? Who the hell do you think you are?"

"Your invitation, sir!"

Reluctantly, he reached into his pocket and pulled out a crumpled piece of card. She appeared to study it closely.

"Thank you for your cooperation, sir." He walked away, his back stiff.

Dave turned to her. "What the fuck is going on, Ariana? What was that all about?"

"Keep it down, Dave."

"Well, Ariana?"

"His invitation says he is Sir Angus Densly. I don't think that's true. I read character, Colin. He is lying. He may be no more than a socialite gate-crasher, but I think you should follow him around, Dave. Colin, we should appear like a couple, which will allow us to move more freely among the guests."

"And when did you get to be the one giving the orders?"

"She's right, Dave. If you get to speak to the boss, ask him if he knows who the guy is."

Dave stomped off towards a position where he could observe the imposter. The rest of the weekend went without incident. On Monday, Ariana would have to sit with Clarant and go through the photos, giving her opinions. Harmless enough maybe but, until she discovered Clarant's purpose, she would be cautious about what she told him.

Chapter 20

Denfar and Itana had left soon after Rosa and Narsin. Tara sat opposite Rafael.

"How are we going to handle this, Tara?"

"I really don't know. I guess we will have to take it one day at a time. Let's see what Meldrum has to say."

The next day they arrived at Meldrum and Konia's rooms together but, before they had time to settle, Tara felt the call of the Guardian. It seemed that Meldrum and Rafael heard it too. Rafael looked a bit confused.

"It's the Guardian of the woods calling us, Rafael. We must go at once."

When they arrived at the woods, it was showing all the signs of early Spring. Leaves were uncurling and sap was rising. There was a feeling of renewal in the air.

They sat in a semi-circle in front of the Guardian Oak.

Tara looked as if she was in a trance when she spoke to Meldrum.

"Show Rafael how to watch over me when I'm gone."

Rafael turned to look at Meldrum, who nodded. When he turned back to Tara, he could see she was not there. Somehow he knew that she had left her body. He began to panic, until Meldrum caught his arm and explained that she was perfectly safe; it was his job to make sure she had a body to return to.

~

Tara found herself back on the edge of the escarpment.

"You have found the one who will watch over you."

Tara turned to see the Guardian, who once again appeared as a young Pixsan woman.

"Now we can teach you how to walk in the Strange. Your experiences here will be real, and you can die here, just as you can in the Familiar. You will be able to travel and observe what is happening in the Familiar world. First, you must know there is no south or north in the Strange. You must be able to visualise where you want to go and who you want to observe.

"There are bad spirits here, agents of your enemy who would destroy you. They can easily deceive. Trust to nothing and, if in doubt, retreat to your own world. Come every morning with your watcher and we will show you how to travel and the dangers you might face. You are our ally and one who will help reforest the world that Cernounos would destroy."

Before she returned, Tara remembered Ariana and asked if the Dryad could help. The Guardian explained that they did not know her; if she brought someone who knew her well, they might be able to find her pattern. It would have to be someone strong in the Talent who was favoured by the Dryad. An image of Rosa popped into Tara's mind. She would bring Rosa with them the following morning.

When they got back, Meldrum asked her to recount every detail. As she spoke, she could see that Rafael was listening intently to everything she was saying, then Meldrum turned to Rafael. "And you, Rafael, what did you experience?"

"It was strange. I was fully aware of everything around me and I could hear and feel every breath Tara took. It was like the wood was watching over me, ready to lend me strength."

~

On the following morning, four of them sat at the foot of the Guardian Oak.

Rosa and Tara had slipped into the trance-like state which Rafael had observed the previous day. Rosa stood and moved to the centre of the three. Thin tree roots appeared from the ground and spiralled up around her until she was completely covered in brown and white tendrils. Minutes passed, and Rafael could feel the tension in Narsin. Slowly, the roots began to sink back into the ground. Tara came back to her body and Rosa awoke to feel Narsin's arms around her.

"All is well, Narsin. It is few who come so close to knowing the Dryad and to enter the Strange. Today, I did both.

"They know Ariana now, Rosa. We must wait for the Dryad to locate her. When they do, I will walk the Strange and see if I can get a message to her." Tara signalled for Rafael to help her up and the four walked back to the farm.

Chapter 21

"What's going on, Itana? You have been flirting outrageously with every single male and female here."

"It doesn't matter, Tara; they all ignore me anyway. They think he owns me, but he damn well doesn't. Just because I'm stuck with him doesn't mean he has any right to control me. I can tell by the way people look at me when I'm with him. They think me an appendage to that damn man."

"Have you talked to him?"

"I am not in the mood to talk to him. I didn't ask for this. He will try and make me see reason. Well, I don't want to see bloody reason. How is reason going to help, when I'm forced to trundle around after him awaiting his call? I did not choose this, and I definitely did not choose him."

Meldrum had asked Tara to tackle Itana about her behaviour and find out what was going on. She volunteered at once; she was regretting it now.

"Will you talk to Rafael about it? After all, he is in the same position as you."

"Are you mad, Tara? Haven't you seen how doe-eyed he's been around you lately?"

"No, I haven't, and I think you should talk to him. Maybe if you can't talk to Denfar about it, he can. At least then you will know how Denfar feels."

"Denfar feels nothing. He treats me the same as before: just some other person to help him. Some woman he needs to draw strength from occasionally. I am no more to him than you or Rafael."

Itana burst into tears. "Go back to Rafael, Tara. I really don't want to talk about this anymore."

~

Denfar had walked up to the garden to meet Rafael at the time he finished work.

He was looking his cool, indifferent self, but Rafael could feel that he was troubled.

"Can we walk and talk, Rafael?"

"Certainly; what's troubling you? No, stop! I know what's troubling you. Tell me how you feel about it."

"It's Itana. She freezes every time we are together. In our training sessions with the elders, she does everything she is asked to. As soon as we leave, I might as well not be there. You have seen how she is in the evenings. She sits as far away as she can from me and listens intently to what I say. She never comments, but I am always waiting for her to contradict me. It's like she's judging me. Then she flirts with everyone in sight. I just don't get it. She is Pixsan. Surely we can work together without all this."

"How do you feel about Itana?"

The big man stopped and turned to Rafael. Blushing, he answered, "I have loved her since I first set eyes on her in your rooms."

Rafael just stood there, hardly believing his ears. The tall, quiet, burly Denfar was in love with Itana, the hot-headed Pixsan from Spain.

"Can you keep what I said to yourself? It is obvious that Itana hates me, so I do not want to make a fool of myself."

"You've made no attempt to explain to her how you feel?"

"You know how she is. It's going to be maddening working with her."

~

Rafael had avoided giving his word to Denfar because he knew he would have to talk to Tara about it.

When he got back, and had washed and cleaned up, he was surprised to find that Tara had cooked something for them both.

"We are going to have to find a new source of mead wine somehow. We are always close to using up all our ration."

Rafael reached for the bottle and poured two glasses.

"Itana is not coming this evening, and I don't think Denfar is either, so I thought I would cook for us instead of us going to family-meal. We do have a few things we need to talk about."

"Thank you. What's going on with Itana? Do you know?"

"I am not sure. Itana resents Denfar; says he thinks he owns her and treats her like an appendage. I am sure that beneath her anger there is something else going on. She says he feels nothing for her, sees her as just some woman he needs to draw power from occasionally."

Rafael laughed; he could not help himself.

"What?" said an annoyed Tara. "She is hurting and all you can do is laugh!"

"Listen, Tara – Denfar met me on my way back today. He is as upset as Itana. He cannot understand the way she has been acting lately. He seemed really miserable.

"I asked him how he felt about her and he asked me not to tell anyone as he did not want to make a fool of himself. Tara, Denfar told me he is in love with her and has loved her since he first set eyes on her."

"What! Are you sure?"

"Absolutely."

Tara just could not believe it. She had watched them when they had been together and Denfar had not shown a single sign of affection towards Itana. What would Itana do if she knew! Tara hated being in this position.

"Do you think I should tell her?"

"Yes – even if she does not share his feelings, she needs to know he holds her in high regard."

"My appetite is gone; let's eat as much as we can and go. If we don't do it now, we will find lots of reasons not to."

They found Itana in her room. She looked really tired. Her eyes were red and she seemed drained. After she'd let them in, she just stood with her back to the wall, one foot crooked behind her.

"Rafael, tell Itana what you told me earlier."

He nodded, but could not help feeling that he was betraying his friend.

When he had finished, they both looked at Itana. Her expression had not changed; she just stood there looking even more miserable.

"Can you just go now."

Rafael felt a bit angry at her response. Tara put a hand on his shoulder.

"Just go, please!"

They stood up and left without looking back.

~

The next morning at their training session, they thought Meldrum looked rather tired.

"I want you to go with Narsin to the Guardian today. I have done all I can for you, Tara. The Guardian will teach you what you need to know. Remember – always snap back into yourself if you sense deception. Know that in the Strange the good can look ugly and the evil handsome."

~

It was not hard for Rafael and Tara to fall into a routine. They got on well and were friends. Tara looked hard for the doe-eyed Rafael that Itana had mentioned, but she could see no sign of it. They still needed a quiet time to talk but, while missing one family-meal was permissible, missing two was frowned upon.

After they were seated in the meal room, they looked around for Itana and Denfar. The two were sat in their usual places talking to the people next to them. Neither looked across the table at the other. At the end of the meal, Rosa stood and welcomed two new students. Then she looked down the table at Rafael.

"Rafael, it is the duty of every Pixsan sworn to the Tort Mae to act as a Caution to those who have declared. You have been called to this duty and you must report any breech to the Tort Mae once the couple has sworn. Do you accept?"

Rafael looked around, feeling a bit bemused. Why had he been chosen? He didn't know, but understood he would have to perform this duty. He voiced his acceptance. Rosa thanked him. Looking down the table she announced, "Denfar has sworn to Itana and Itana has sworn to Denfar. They are Declared."

There was a stunned silence around the table, then, one by one, those gathered started to bang the table with wooden spoons to show their approval.

They saw little of Denfar and Itana in the days that followed. Meldrum was keen for Tara to visit the Guardian every day to seek news. It was over a week before Tara could report back to Meldrum that the Dryad had located Ariana. It seemed she was being held somewhere in Somerset.

The Dryad had planted an image of a large country house in Tara's head. Konia set to work dragging up images on the computer of every documented country house in the county. Tara stopped Konia when an image of Clerkendale Manor appeared on the screen. They read the information that came with the image and discovered that Clerkendale Manor was owned by Gregory Clarant. They found a short biography: Member of Parliament, moneyed and founder of the far-right party, Britain First. Tara recognised him as the man on the train.

"It seems he is powerful, influential and very wealthy. I think he is dangerous. Tara, can you contact Ariana?"

"I will go tomorrow to see if there is a way."

Meldrum caught Tara's hand as she stood to go.

"I don't know what you said to Itana and Denfar, but you have made my life a lot easier. They came the evening before they Declared. I have many skills, Tara, but relationship counsellor is not one of them. I told them of my past and stressed they must obey the rules. Not just you, Rafael; every one of us will be watching them. I think the Tort Mae will not be easy on them if they fail to comply. Tara, seek her out; they will need every distraction they can get. Now, you two – how are you coping?"

They looked at each other, but said nothing.

"Very well; I will not ask again."

Chapter 22

Konia and Meldrum stayed up late that night and printed off every detail they could find about Clarant. His wealth, time in the city financial sector and disregard for others all indicated a man obsessed with power.

The next day, they shared the information they had collected with Rosa and Narsin.

"Cernounos must have made him aware of Talent holders. It must be the reason he has taken Ariana. Josie and Anna have captured a Talent sensitive and are holding him at the Refuge. He must be Clarant's man. At last we have some pieces fitting together. If this Clarant thinks they are holding him, they could send armed men into the Refuge, but I don't think it will be so easy for them this time, with Josie and Anna being there."

"We'll leave for the city and the Refuge today."

Meldrum looked over at Rosa with a smile. "Be careful."

When they arrived at the Refuge, they found Gary in a state of high anxiety.

"I'm so glad you're here. Josie and Anna are keeping watch over him in the basement. They tell me he is quite strong in his Talent, but it's the only one he has. Since he has been confined, he has stopped eating and is growing weak. They try their best, but I think they have no idea what to do next. I really hate having someone confined here against their will."

"Take us to him, Gary."

They walked down the stairs to the basement. Josie met them on the way.

"Anna is inside with him. He knows we are powerful, but he has no idea which one of us trapped him in air. He's refusing to eat. What do you think? Take his memory or his Talent?"

"I will need to see him."

Rosa opened the door, and before them was a young guy around twenty-five. He wore jeans and a T-shirt with a small Britain First logo on it. The air smelt of sweat. He was tall and very slim, too much so for his height. He turned his gaunt face towards them.

"Guess I chose the wrong side."

Narsin looked across at him.

"Side?"

"My boss sent me to look out for people like you. I thought I was clever when I saw the black-haired woman come. She had an aura – something... I don't know, so I informed the boss and they came for her. Then they turned up." He pointed to Josie and Anna. "I thought the black-haired woman was powerful, but these two – shit! They just took me so easy. Now you," he said, looking directly at Rosa. "Fuck, man – I swear I had no idea what I was getting into."

Narsin spoke quietly to him.

"We are sorry for you, but you have been corrupted by Cernounos and we cannot offer you sanctuary."

The guy looked up pleadingly.

"I've had enough of all this. Can you make me normal? Please, please say you can."

~ 101 ~

Rosa reached into his mind and took out his Talent. There was no pain to her; it was a request. They opened the door and let him go. Just before he reached reception, Josie reached out and took away his memories.

Narsin held onto Rosa as she coped with what had happened. Josie just shrugged.

"If we hadn't caught the arrogant little sod, right opposite the front door, the lanky bastard would have been no end of trouble. Shit, Rosa, if I hadn't taken his memories he could have been an open book to our enemy."

"I know, I know. Now we need to talk to Gary. The Refuge must close as soon as possible. We cannot risk a fight with armed men here. Can you stay with Sarah for a while so there is no trace of Talent here? But stay in constant contact with Father Gary."

"What are you going to do?"

"We will go now and set up the cottage at Woolacombe Down for any of Gary's clients who might have Talent. He must refer the rest to Social Services. Then he must come to us."

The next few days were hectic ones for Gary as he began to close the Refuge. He was relieved when the last of his clients left. Rosa and Narsin had taken the two undamaged Talents back to Devon and removed the conflicts of the Others. He had just locked up and was heading for the car park when he noticed a big black BMW parked opposite. He hurried across to unlock the gate. He rang Josie, and Anna answered. He told her quickly what was happening. Josie took the phone.

"Drive via the roundabout at the bottom of Ash Hill. Look in your mirror as you go up the hill and, as soon as you see the black BMW, come to a halt on the roundabout; go as quickly as you can to Horfield Common. Park behind the parish church out of sight of the road."

Gary drove out of the car park, quickly turning left away from the direction the black car was facing. He drove onto the M24, constantly checking his rear-view mirror, and then took the slip road to the San Paulo roundabout. Here, he took the third exit to Ash Hill. Josie was standing 50 yards up the hill at the side of the road. When Gary arrived at the mini roundabout, where traffic joined from St Werburgh's, he could see the BMW not far behind. It had to stop and wait as a car had pulled onto the roundabout from the right. As soon as the BMW was on the roundabout and blocking the entrance from St Werburgh's, Josie struck. The BMW stalled. She could hear the driver's frantic attempts to get it started and the horns of the cars which had started to back up on the other two entrance roads. Gary accelerated up the hill and, as he passed Sarah's road, he saw Josie and Anna's old camper van pulling out. They met up on Horfield Common, where they parked alongside one another.

"What will you do now, Gary?"

"I am going to head on up to Oxford for a while to stay with Janice and her partner. They are always asking me to visit; I will ring them now before I set off. I am sure there are lots of parishes which need a temporary priest, so I will be travelling around until it is safe to return and open the Refuge."

They wished each other safe journeys and headed off on their separate ways.

Chapter 23

Ariana was sitting at a table with Colin and Clarant in the room at the end of the terrace.

"How did you know about the imposter, Ariana?"

"Intuition; everything about him told me he was a liar. Not easy to explain, I know. Anyway, who else did you want me to tell you about?"

"He was an imposter, but not that much to worry about. He is Angus Densley's younger brother."

He placed a photo in front of Ariana. It was of the couple she had first spotted. The obese man and the blonde woman.

"Never mind the woman, Ariana; we all know what motivates her. The man, Ariana: what motivates him?"

"He was quite difficult to read; he has some skill in that. He is calculating, quite cold, cares little about anyone, even his partner. Treacherous, I'd say, but only in the last resort. I would not want to go into business with him."

Clarant placed another photo on the table. She recognised the woman, a brunette, quite plain, unremarkable at first glance, but there was more to her than to the man.

"He is quite even in temperament, thinks things through, but she is the decision-maker. He would do nothing without talking to her first. Once a decision is made he will stick with it. Not loyal nor treacherous, but committed."

They went through a couple more, and Clarant called it a day.

"Thank you, Ariana. Now, you said there would be a price."

"I need to exercise: I need access to the grounds to walk and run. Colin can come with me, and Rex, for an hour in the morning."

"Ariana, you pose a problem for me. I will be honest, Colin has a certain Talent, but he feels it does not work on you. Rex and Nick, yes; you, no. How can I trust you?"

"You can't, Gregory, but you can give Dave a gun and if I run for it he can shoot me in the leg," she said, laughing. "Look, Gregory, I have been a farm hand and a live-in volunteer at a refuge; this job is not so bad. The food is good and I don't have to pay rent. I have Rex to play chess with, and Nick to annoy me. I have no family, so I might as well stay here where my Talent is appreciated."

"OK, Ariana, but Dave will be watching you. You can run with the men at nine each morning."

~

On her first run, Ariana tripped and fell near the big oak. Rex came back for her. She sat with her knees pulled up and her head down on them.

"You OK?"

"Yes, yes; tripped over that bloody root."

"Let's run, then."

She pulled herself up using the trunk of the old oak for support. By this time, Nick had come back to join them. Dave shouted from the terrace that their time was up, and to get back.

Chapter 24

Tara awoke from the Strange to find Rafael staring at her.

"You're back, thank the spirits."

"You have no need to worry, Rafael. I can pull myself back to my body if I feel I am in danger. The Dryads tell me if I only enter the Strange when I have a mission to complete, it is unlikely I will be noticed. They tell me not to linger and I have no intentions of doing so. It is a very seductive place; I have been warned to spend no more time there than I need to. Now, I have news from Ariana. We must go and find Rosa and Narsin."

Rosa and Narsin were still teaching, so they went to see Meldrum and Konia. Meldrum suggested they wait for Rosa and Narsin so that Tara did not have to repeat herself.

Meldrum asked Rafael how he thought Denfar and Itana were coping. Rafael told her that Denfar was determined to hold to his vow. He had also spoken to Itana, who had told him the same. She would not risk the period of Caution being extended."

"You are right; I think the love they never thought they had will guide them. They will not risk the disfavour of the Tort Mae."

When Rosa and Narsin had joined them in Konia's study, Tara explained that she had waited in a large oak in the grounds. Ariana was out running and sensed her presence. She is staying to find out what Clarant is up to. Tara repeated everything that Ariana had been able to pass on to her in their short period of contact.

"She can call the Dryads now they know her; they will call me if Ariana wants to make contact again."

"I think we need to call the Tort Mae so that you can report to them directly. We must try and anticipate what Clarant will do. They will also need to approve the Caution we have given Denfar and Itana."

~

That evening, Denfar and Itana came to the woodshed. They sat apart as if nothing had happened, but their smiles gave them away.

"I want to thank you, Rafael, for betraying my trust."

"My pleasure, Denfar. When people are blind to things, someone has to make them see."

Itana laughed. "And you, Tara – have the scales fallen from your eyes?"

"I'm sure I don't know what you're talking about."

"Your denial is unconvincing. Look, you can see the disappointment on dear Rafael's face."

"Stop it, Itana! Denfar, you have a hard life in front of you."

For the first time since they'd met, they heard the sound of Denfar's laughter. "It would be a much harder life without her."

Chapter 25

Ariana was developing a strong friendship with Rex. She had made it clear that she was not interested in him in any other way, and he had the sense to accept this. Nick was another matter; he was annoying. She was not quite sure how to deal with him.

Rex told her about another man that had been there, called John. They had questioned him for days and then he suddenly disappeared. Ariana was beginning to think the same thing might happen to Nick. It was obvious to her that he knew nothing of his ex-girlfriend's whereabouts. When Clarant asked her about Nick, she claimed he had some latent ability, but was not sure what it was. As a result, Clarant kept him on.

From his side, Rex had become fiercely loyal to Ariana. He knew that harbouring romantic notions about her was a waste of time. He sensed that whatever Talent he had, Ariana had it multiplied a thousand times. She had hinted she could help him and that she could get them out of their prison. He believed her. In his mind, she was someone who personified the meaning of cool.

They were sat together playing yet another game of chess when Colin came for Ariana. It had got to the stage where Ariana could smell Colin's aftershave before he reached the door. Always the same one, with that chemical smell she disliked. Since she had been away from the Pixsan community, and among men who used such things, she had often pondered why any woman would be attracted by it.

Colin beckoned for her to follow him, and they took the familiar path up to the terrace room.

"We have another important weekend before us, my dear. Colin will partner you, so you look like a couple. Should the need arise, you can once again claim you are security. David will be keeping an eye on you from a distance. You will judge the character of the people Colin points out to you."

"And…"

"And what, my dear?"

Ariana always cringed at his patronising use of the phrase 'my dear'.

"Look, Clarant, I have done nothing but work at everything you have asked, yet I am still locked up in the basement. Employ me and I could help even more. Rex is very loyal to me and I could find a use for Nick. Employ us and you will have a good security team. Let us wander freely in the grounds. As a team, we could be useful in many ways."

"Let me think on it, my dear."

Clarant dismissed her and nodded to Colin, indicating that she should find her own way back to the basement.

~

Clarant was worried; there had been no sign of the spirit for months. It had been present in the early days, when it had helped him recruit his first Talents. It seemed absent now. Clarant did not understand Cernounos. It was a creature who used the weakness of otherwise intelligent people against themselves. However, Cernounos had no doubt that Gregory Clarant would feed its hunger for human grief. There was no need to interfere more than necessary.

Cernounos was unaware of a Pixsan right in the middle of the conspiracy he had set in progress. The Pixsan had become allies with many spirits and each House had its own. There was no earth spirit as dangerous as Cernounos, but there were still other tricksters out there. All Pixsan had been taught how to hide from them. Ariana could only be recognised by another Pixsan.

~

Rex was getting more and more anxious, while Nick was drifting along in his own weird denial. Nick was volatile, and Ariana knew that if he became more so he would have to be sacrificed.

They were sitting at the chess board.

"Why do you think you are here, Rex?"

Rex knew, but had never wanted to think about it too deeply. In her quiet way, Ariana made him realise it was important he did. It was also important she knew. He felt he had to be honest with her.

"Do you know how much shit I am carrying, Ariana?"

"No."

"Well, when not much more than a kid, I thought I was 'the man'. I became involved with a group using the Internet and phone calls to scam people out of their life savings. I was good at it. Never thought about the people whose lives I was ruining. I felt I could do anything, but the lessons that prison teaches you soon put me right. Some clever tech head, working for the police, tracked us down. They had recordings of my phone calls to female victims. Truth is, the real lessons started here.

"Some men struggle to attract women. I had no problems. I thought I had the golden touch, but one day Dave was in a vindictive mood and put me right. He said I had a minor Compulsive Talent, which was nothing compared to his own. It was the Talent that allowed me to talk women into bed and without it they wouldn't have given me a second glance.

"This led me to thinking about how much of my life had been a fraud. I did fall for one woman, the one they are always asking me about. She was strong, and I guess she was the first one I was really interested in. But I couldn't change my ways, and one day I got home to find her wardrobe empty. She didn't stay to talk about it, just disappeared. They keep pumping me for information about her; they must have realised by now that I have no idea where she is. I think they're just keeping me here as a companion for you. They haven't worked it out, but I think you could leave any time you wanted and I am counting on you to take me with you."

"Let's not get too far ahead, Rex. At the moment, I am trying to talk Clarant into employing us as his security. He is beginning to trust me, but I need to work on him a bit more. I worry about Nick. I am going to try and arrange his escape. I am staying for a while. You can go with him if you want; it's up to you."

"I don't know how you are going to get that skinny twat out, but I know you can do it. I won't be going with him. You need someone to cover your back and that's gonna be me."

"OK, just show surprise when they can't find him. It'll be easier for us if he is out of the way."

~

When the weekend arrived, Colin came for Ariana. Gregory Clarant was waiting in the usual room off the terrace. It smelt less musty than normal, and the paintings of his ancestors had been rearranged to accommodate one of Gregory himself. He was standing, making his maiden speech in the House of Commons. The red-covered seats stood out against the browns and greys of the building's interior. It fitted with the stuffy portraits of formally dressed men that surrounded the room.

Clarant pointed to the table where a dozen or so photographs were laid out.

"Do you recognise any of these people, Ariana?"

Ariana looked at all the photos carefully. She had been taking a special interest in the news since the last weekend gathering.

"Only that one. Isn't that one of the Prime Minister's closest advisors, Don Yendo?"

"Yes Ariana, that's exactly who it is. I will be talking to him a lot of the time and I want you to see how he reacts. The rest of them are not so important, apart form these two."

He pointed to the images of two men. They were of similar height and unremarkable in appearance. She thought she might have caught sight of one of them on TV, perhaps on the news broadcast about the Treasury announcing new interest rates.

~

Ariana was on the terrace with Colin as the guests began to arrive. She watched as Clarant greeted them all individually. He showed no special favour to anyone, and spent equal time talking to new arrivals as they became familiar with their surroundings and the other guests.

Lunch was served buffet style, with catering staff moving through the guests carrying trays of drinks. She had spotted Don Yendo the minute he got out of his car. He was the last to arrive. Everyone there was dressed formally except for him. He was slim and slightly hunched. His hair was thin and short. He wore large, black-framed spectacles which rested on a large nose. She felt his scruffy appearance was not deliberate: it was just that he cared very little about it.

Clarant headed straight for him as soon as he realised he was there. They clasped each other in brotherly fashion and immediately began to talk. Just pleasantries, she thought; the real conversation would take place later that night.

Yendo was a mystery to most people. How he had become indispensable to the Prime Minister nobody knew. Many of the political commentators thought the current PM so weak that he could not operate without people like Yendo.

Colin had taken a loo break and left Ariana quietly watching the guests, when the Treasury man appeared at her side. She turned to face him.

"Can I help you, sir?"

"Sir?"

"I am part of the security team, sir; if you would allow, I cannot be distracted."

"Ah yes, that would explain your interest in Don."

"Please, sir, if you have any doubts about my presence do speak to Sir Gregory."

"Problems, Ariana?"

Colin had returned and took up his position beside her.

"No, Colin, Mr... um..."

"Carney, James Carney."

"Mr Carney was a little concerned about me."

"Sir, I can vouch for Ariana; she is a loyal servant of Sir Clarant and has his trust. She is soon to be appointed head of security." Ariana gave Colin a quizzical look.

"Forgive me, madam, it seems we share an occupation which gives us curious and sceptical minds."

"Forgiveness is not in order, sir; we have duties, and if you would allow?"

She nodded and signalled Colin to follow her. She was careful not to mention Colin's slip about her coming promotion.

"Let's move to where I can see the other guests."

~

When Ariana got back to the basement she warned Rex that it was now a matter of urgency for Nick to disappear. "You will know nothing of it when it happens, so their Compulsion will be of no consequence. I am sorry, Rex, but – for your protection – you may suffer a little forgetfulness."

~

Ariana was called to see Clarant on Monday morning at the usual time.

"Well, Ariana, what about Yendo?"

"Complex, a bully to those he has control over, and manipulator of those who are his equals and within his influence. A maverick, the press might call him, but I sensed at his centre he is insecure. His weakness is that he likes to be liked. He provokes people all the time to test their loyalty. He is dangerous and unpredictable and to be avoided in business. An all-out winner or loser who finds compromise very difficult."

"And the other two?"

"MI5, or whatever name they go under now. They were here solely to protect him."

They discussed the other guests, and Clarant was quite surprised when Ariana told him that one of the guests was asking questions that were too pointed.

"She is a journalist, but I thought her a tame one. She will be off the guest list in future. Thank you, Ariana. Oh, one other thing: I have been thinking of your proposal and will let you know in the coming week what I have decided." Ariana nodded and left to find her own way back to the basement.

Chapter 26

Nick's head was spinning. He looked around, tried to focus but couldn't. A voice came from nearby. "You OK? You look a mess." Nick was too woozy; he just couldn't summon a coherent answer. He realised he stank and was covered in something sticky. "Looks like you came off your bike and ended up in the ditch."

Nick looked around and he could just about make out a hedgerow with a ditch running alongside it. On the bank lay a bicycle with a crumpled front wheel. As Nick's head began to clear he saw two women standing close to him.

"I think we better get you to hospital; you might be concussed."

Nick tried to speak, but he couldn't find any words, so they helped him into the van and drove him towards Bristol and the A&E of its largest hospital.

When they arrived, there were loads of questions about how the women found him. Did they see the accident and was there a vehicle involved? The medics were suspicious and called the police, who asked similar questions and examined the camper van. They checked on their handheld computer and found it was registered to Anna at the Woolacombe Cottage, just as she said. In the end, they were convinced by the women's Good Samaritan story and sent them on their way. They left Nick in the care of the head injuries unit. Josie and Anna got in the van and started the drive back to Devon.

~

Ariana had asked the Dryad to call Tara and explain to her about Nick. Josie and Anna had volunteered to carry out the rescue. Josie had lifted the perimeter wire to let Anna in. They had waited for Ariana and Rex to run past, and Josie hit Nick with a ball of air, knocking him unconscious. Anna ran from the bushes where she had been hiding and dragged Nick to the fence. Josie lifted the fencing without breaking it and they dragged him to the van. After bundling him in, they headed for the road where they had set up the fake accident.

"What will happen to him now?" asked Anna.

"I tried to be as careful as I could with his memory, but I lack the skill of Ariana. He will gain some of it back in a few days and the hospital will contact his family or social services. I'm not sure what will happen after that, but he will not have a clear memory of his time at Clarant's. I am not sure about his Talent. Ariana may have removed it just before I knocked him out."

"There are many security cameras at Clerkendale Manor, but most surround the house and gardens. There are none in the old deer park where the basement dwellers go for their daily run. The deer park is surrounded by a high wire fence to discourage poachers. Clarant never worried about his captors running from there until now."

~

When Ariana and Rex returned form the morning run, Nick was not with them. Dave wanted to know where he was and, when it was clear he was not following on, Dave raised the alarm. Clarant came around the corner in his

Land Rover with two of his dogs in the back and called for Dave to jump in.

"Talk to them, Colin," he shouted. "I want to know exactly what happened."

Colin turned to Rex.

"Tell me, where he is? It will save you a lot of trouble later."

Ariana could see that he was using the full force of his Compulsive Talent.

Rex shrugged. "How am I to know what that skinny little twat is up to? It's annoying enough I have to share some space with him."

Colin could feel that Rex knew nothing. He turned to Ariana. "And you, you pride yourself as a judge of character; what do you think has happened?"

"I told Clarant I thought he was hiding something, but I didn't know what. He's obviously had something up his sleeve and was just waiting his chance."

Rex laughed. "Who'd have thought the little squirt could have been scheming to get out all along. He has been carrying out a bloody good act if he has."

Just then the Land Rover came screeching to a halt alongside the terrace, with the dogs running in behind it.

"No sign of him. Colin, in my office now! I will talk to you two later."

Ariana and Rex went back down to the basement. As soon as they were inside, Rex asked what was going on.

"Don't ask, Rex. In the words of the old proverb, what you don't know won't hurt you. Trust me for now."

They settled down to a game of chess and waited.

Without knowing it, Rex was learning a great deal from Ariana. He'd stopped obsessing about getting out and gained a calmness he had never felt before. He always needed to be doing something and was bemused at Ariana's ability to remain still. He asked her about it, and she had told him he should not overthink everything, just be still and use the time to think, to think slowly and methodically. "Then, when the time comes to act, you will be ready. It's like chess," she told him. He knew he would never fully understand Ariana, but he was determined to try.

There had always been a phone on the wall inside the entrance of the basement. It had never rung and nobody had picked up the receiver as it was assumed such old technology didn't work. Now it rang, and Ariana realised it was part of a domestic system. She nodded to Rex, who took his time answering. He was silent for a while, listening, and then spoke into the phone. "OK, sir, I will bring Ariana now."

"Rex, are you my new keeper?" she said smiling.

"As if, just let a man appear a bit tough every now and then, Ariana."

"OK, team leader," she replied, with a big smile on her face. "Lead on."

When they arrived in the terrace room, only Clarant and Colin were there. Clarant was silent for a while. He looked at Rex and then Ariana.

"Are you two partners?"

Rex looked across at Ariana, but before Ariana could speak Rex replied yes.

"I see, so if I employ one of you I employ both?"

"You do."

"And what do you say, Ariana?"

"We are a team, Rex and I. We could help in many ways."

"I see. You did warn me that Nick was more than he appeared, but I paid no attention. Neither Colin nor Dave spotted anything. The fact that you are still here means you were not involved. You have been loyal, Ariana, and you have given me trust in Rex. Dave has been sent to Bristol to see if he can locate Nick. I fear your assessment of him being more loyal to money than to me is probably correct.

"Ariana, I am taking a risk on you, but risk-taking is something I've always been good at. You will head up security here. I want your candid analysis about the house and grounds.

"Rex, I know all about your background, and I guess you will be invaluable to us. I want you to cast aside any resentment you have towards Colin and work with him closely. You will have free run of the grounds. For now you will have the basement to yourselves. Well?"

Ariana looked across at Rex. He nodded.

"Thank you, Gregory, or must we stick to Sir Clarant?"

"In private, Gregory will do, but I know you will act appropriately in any social situation that arises."

"Well, Gregory, we will examine the boundaries tomorrow. We do not require Internet or smartphones; access to Internet TV will help us to keep abreast of news. We do not know or want to know your business, but we need to be aware of what's happening in the world.

Sometimes knowing a single thread can allow one to pull a carpet apart."

Clarant nodded. "I will get something organised for you. I will be setting up some important meetings soon. I want you to be at them, Ariana, so that that you can access the responses to my proposals. Rex, for now, you will be taking Dave's place. Colin will brief you on what is needed. I want to keep Dave in Bristol for a while.

"Now, tell me, Ariana, were there any other Talent-bearers at the Refuge?"

"None that I know of. Father Gary is a perceptive and caring priest, and he takes in all and sundry. His funding has been sketchy though," she lied, "and I was expecting it to close at any time."

"I see. Well, I'll brief you soon about the upcoming meetings."

They knew they had been dismissed, so headed back to the basement.

Chapter 27

Meldrum was sat with Konia. She was reading local Somerset newspapers on the 'net to see if there was anything concerning Clarant. Konia was lost in a book which he thought Tara should read. They were not surprised when a pigeon flew through the open window. Meldrum stood and removed the small canister that was attached to its leg. Inside was a message from Corrin.

The message explained that he was not really worried and the women at the House of the Mer were not worried either, but now Charly had reached her third trimester could Meldrum come and check all was well. He did add that all the local women had told him not to bother her.

Meldrum thought about it while the pigeon perched patiently.

"I do not know what you think, Konia, but I know that Denfar has the healing skills of old. He absorbs herb lore faster than I can provide it. His mother was the midwife in his community and he tells me he followed her everywhere, even as a toddler. Male healers are rare. Even more so, those who are Talent-bearers. There are only two in the Histories who I can think of, and neither of them had an amplifier."

"What are you saying, Meldrum?"

"I am saying that Denfar, not I, should go to the House of the Mer with Itana, and that Tara and Rafael should accompany them. While they are there they can take a look at the medicine garden that Corrin tells us they are developing. Perhaps Rafael and Denfar can offer them some advice."

The next day, Orita led Denfar and the others across the moor and along the coast towards the House of the Mer. Their five horses travelled in single file down the narrow coast road until they reached what looked like an old muddy lane.

"This is the path you must take. Do not be deceived by its appearance. When you come in sight of the Rookery, dismount, for as soon as the Rooks see you they will set about squawking to alert Corrin. You will need to calm the horses. Corrin or one of the others will meet you at the Rookery and invite you to the House. Do not proceed further until you have been invited. This is important."

The Pixsan understood this, but Tara was a bit bemused. Orita saw her confusion and promised to explain why it was important at their next talk about the Histories.

The four left Orita at the crossroads and headed down the track. As soon as they had left the narrow entrance, the track broadened out into a road metalled with large flat stones. There was something about this path which induced a feeling of foreboding in Tara. The others didn't seem to notice anything. Little was said until the Rookery came into view. They quickly dismounted and walked forward. On the tallest branch of the ash grove a lone rook perched. As soon as he saw them he started to caw and all the others joined in. They held on tightly to the horses' reins and waited.

Suddenly all went quiet and they noticed a tall, thin man walking up the lane. He was dressed in Pixsan white and had a long straggly beard. He stopped a few feet away, and a dunnock flew down and sat on his shoulder.

"Welcome all. You are invited to the House of the Mer. Do you accept?"

They all answered in the affirmative and a broad smile spread across his face.

"I am Corrin, life partner to Charly. Follow me; it is time for mid-meal and there you will meet Charly and the rest of our family."

As they walked down the combe, Tara began to smell the salty air of the sea. She began to take note of her surroundings. The combe was narrow with high, thickly wooded hills of beech, ash and oak on either side. The lane was steep and had been cut in zigzag fashion to take the strain out of the journey back up to the road. As they approached the sea, the combe opened out. On the left, she could see buildings set around a square. The ones at the back seemed to be cut into the hillside and Tara could see little windows high up, indicating there was more than one storey inside.

To the right was a steep cliff face that extended out into the sea. What looked like a pier was being built alongside it. There were workshops, and Tara thought she could hear the sound of machinery. As they came out of the lane, Tara could see a large building to her immediate right. It looked like it had been a grand hotel. It was built in a Swiss style with exposed timbers: definitely Alpine in appearance. They headed across to the square to where Tara thought the meal room would be.

People were gathered outside waiting to enter and slowly started to file in when they arrived. Many were dressed in the Pixsan white she was used to, but others were dressed in everyday work clothes of denim and cotton.

The meal room was much like the one at the farm. Corrin and a tall, striking woman stood at its head. The woman, who she guessed must be Charly, looked down to the foot of the table where the newcomers were sitting. She asked Denfar if he would say the grace.

"Mother of the earth and all its spirits, we thank you for the plants that feed us and the plants that heal us."

Corrin spoke the grace of his House and everyone sat waiting for the food to be served.

Mid-meal never lasted long. When it was over, the four were invited to follow Corrin and Charly to the old hotel. Their rooms were on the first floor. The large French windows of the sitting-room overlooked the beach. Charly asked them to seat themselves.

Looking at Itana, Charly asked, "You have recently been conflicted; are you happy now?"

Looking at Denfar, Itana smiled. "I will be."

"Ah, I see, so you are declared to the Healer here."

Corrin laughed.

"Well, listen you two, the declared have a hard time of it here. Not only do they have to cope with my owls, who patrol the night, but with Charly's Mer sense."

Tara looked over at Charly. "Mer sense?"

"I carried a Mer spirit inside me in my growing years. My Mer sister now swims freely beside me, but I have inherited her sensitivity to human feelings."

"When you say Mer do you..."

Charly interrupted her. "Humans know them by many names. Rafael's people may know them as Sirenas. Almost all of the human myths about them are wrong. Now tell me, Rafael and Tara, are you declared?"

Tara glanced at Rafael, but both remained silent.

"I see. I can sense what is in your hearts, yet only you can truly know. Now, Denfar, my well-meaning partner has called you to make sure I am well. He has done this despite the fact that I can sense my son's wellness, despite the Mer telling me my son is fine and despite the fact that every woman in the village has told him not to waste your time."

Denfar smiled.

"Well, I have no Mer sense, and I am a mere male, but I do have some insight into how confinement works. How do you know the child you bear is a boy?"

"The Mer refer to him as such, as do Corrin's birds. I too sense the maleness of my child."

"Have you suffered any loss of appetite, sickness or faintness?"

"No."

"Have you lost blood?"

"No."

"How often do you swim with the Mer?"

"Every day. When I enter the water, the Mer shroud me so the coldness of the sea does not penetrate my body. They care as much for my child as I."

"Can I listen to your child?"

He put both hands on Charly's belly, then turned to Itana, whose eyes momentarily glazed.

"Your child's heart is strong. You are fit and well. Do not enter the sea unless the Mer are present, as the shock may harm your child. I am sure they will guide you. Listen to your Mer sense. If something feels wrong, call for me."

He turned to Corrin. "My time is never wasted when it comes to the health of a child; you have nothing to worry about."

"Thank you, Denfar, and you too Itana. Now I must show you something we hope will interest you all."

He indicated for them to follow and they headed off towards the beach. Just before they reached it, Corrin led them to a building just beyond the square. Denfar guessed it to be the community's Place Apart as it had two large doors and a smaller human-sized one cut into the one on the left. They entered a large hall and at the far end were doors resembling the ones they had just passed through. Beyond them was a tunnel that had been carved through rock.

Tara could see a small window of daylight some way ahead. At the end of the cave-like tunnel they came out into a combe that had previously been cut off by the sea. It reached back into the hillside. Tara could see that it ended near the base of a steep cliff. It was full of trees which she did not recognise.

Rafael stood next to her, open-mouthed in surprise. Denfar was talking quickly with Itana. Tara could hear him explaining the healing qualities of each tree. There were also glasshouses and herb beds with beehives among them. Corrin explained that Charly had discovered this hidden combe a little while after they had settled there. She had swum up to it and begun to explore.

It was a little while before she came upon the entrance to the cave. Dappled light shone into it from its farthest end. Charly had walked through it, thinking that it might lead back to the House.

When she had called out, she had surprised a pair of youngsters who thought they had found a secluded spot to take a break together.

"I was called and we soon had the trees and shrubs that were hiding the entrance trimmed back. The tunnel must have been cut into the rock by the people who built the hotel, for it is clearly not a natural cave."

It took them a little while to realise what the combe could be used for. It was sheltered from the prevailing south-westerlies and from cold winds from the east. Trees and plants could be grown there which could not be grown elsewhere.

The Mer House was growing in number, but had little to trade with other communities. Most Pixsan disliked fish, which was the one thing they had a plentiful supply of. Their settlement had been funded by the Tort Mae at first; now they needed something to trade for goods and labour.

One of the young women who had answered the call for volunteers to help build the new house was a healer. She had also taken courses at Edinburgh University in Botany and Plant Science. Her name was Terina, one of a growing number of Pixsan resistant to the effects of iron. Terina had planned the medicine garden with Charly. It was early days, but already the trees and plants were establishing well.

The voices of the newcomers had drawn Terina from her work in the glasshouse.

Corrin introduced everyone. Terina hardly had time to draw breath. Questions came at her quick and fast from Denfar and Rafael.

Corrin interceded. "Come now, you can ask Terina all the questions you wish after family-meal tonight. We have guestrooms in the old hotel where you can stay." Looking directly at Itana and smiling, he added, "My owls like to perch there in the eaves; they miss nothing."

"Don't worry, Corrin. I have given my word, and this lump of a man beside me would rather die than face the wrath of the women of the Tort Mae."

That evening they discussed what medicines they could develop and make at the House of the Mer. Not only did they have the resources of the combe but also the plants of the sea. Denfar could see endless opportunities. He was keen to be involved, but all knew the fight against Cernounos must take precedence. The next day they returned to the moorland farm and their training.

Chapter 28

Ariana and Rex settled into a daily pattern. They ran the boundary every morning and evening, played chess, and watched the news looking for anything they might use. Ariana was keen to gather as much information about Don Yendo as she could. She was worried about his hold on the Prime Minister and the influence Clarant had over him. He was strong-willed, but Colin had Talent enough to put suggestions into his mind. Clarant would not have taken an interest in him unless there was some payback. She sensed that money was the main motivator for Clarant, but what and where were his investments? She would ask the Dryad to summon Tara. Konia and Meldrum would soon find out where Clarant's assets lay.

Every few days they would be called by Clarant to report. Ariana was sure Clarant was setting traps for them, so made sure she noticed any changes. Today he looked a little smug, but they were ready.

"Anything to report?"

Whenever she could, she let Rex take the lead. Clarant preferred dealing with males. She guessed he suffered smart women, rather than admired them. Rex spoke up.

"There is something odd at the old ice house out beyond the stables. The door appears to have been forced, but there is no sign of a break-in through the boundary fence. We have checked the CCTV. Have you sent workers to do repairs or estimates for renovation? The damage could only have been done by a staff member."

"You surmise correctly. The key had been lost and I ordered the break-in. I am looking to repurpose the building."

Ariana managed to look bored all the way through the conversation.

"You are both needed this weekend. I had thought about you acting out a role as waiters but, as Yendo's minders will obviously be around, I have decided to put you on the guest list as a couple. You almost look like one, after all," he said, with a disapproving note to his voice.

"That's for the best, as I work much better with Rex at my side."

"We will see, Ariana, we will see. I want Rex to be closely involved with the preparations so he can work directly with Colin. You, Ariana, can assist me."

When they got back to the basement, Rex expressed his concerns.

"That guy is a creep, Ariana, and I hate the way he looks at you. I think he would like to get rid of me."

"Don't worry; over the next few days I will learn more about him and his plans. I am waiting for some information, then we can act."

"And where would you get your information from?"

"Look Rex, I do not want to keep you in the dark, but the less you know the less our friend Colin can know. Just trust me."

Rex wasn't happy, but he knew Ariana would not keep things from him unless it was necessary.

Colin came for Rex the next morning and sent Ariana up to meet Clarant.

"I want to know if you can make judgements from video clips."

"Not so well as when I am in the room. Show me what you want analysed."

He beckoned for her to cross the room to come and sit next to him. She did not sit, but stood behind him where she could look down at the screen. "Show me," she said again. Clarant pressed some keys and a video began on the screen. It was Yendo and the Prime Minister, Keiran Jackstone-Farmer.

The PM sat quietly listening to what Yendo had to say. They were talking about reforms to the labour market. Yendo was arguing that radical change was needed. That everyone who worked should be on a zero hours contract. The economy could not afford sick pay and holiday pay anymore. Times had changed. The PM suggested that these policies would not be popular. There could be social unrest. Yendo argued that the police force needed to be beefed up and this should be accomplished before the reforms. Yendo told him that the miners were defeated by Margaret Thatcher and that any who challenged his reforms should be treated in the same way.

Clarant stopped the video and asked if she thought the PM would act on Yendo's advice. She told him that it was difficult to tell from the video, but she thought that he might. The only thing holding him back would be his desire to be popular.

"He does not appear to be a very deep person. I think he finds complicated ideas difficult to cope with. He needs people he trusts to explain them."

There were a few more videos, some about foreign policy and others about British troops overseas.

"I won't ask how you got this material, Gregory. Politics is of no interest to me, but it seems our PM is very weak and very dependent on Yendo."

"OK, Ariana, now tell me, are you really in a relationship with Rex?"

"Why do you ask?"

"Well, I imagine a future with him might not go far. If, on the other hand, you were partnered with someone like me, your future would be one full of luxury and finery."

"To tell you the truth, Gregory, I have no interest in such things. I have no Dragon Blood in me that makes me crave the accumulation of vast sums of wealth, only to sit on it for fear someone might take it away. My future may not lie with Rex or anyone else; the days are gone when the future of a woman depends upon a man."

She could tell her answer did not go down too well, but she had the information from Gregory she needed and, as soon as Tara contacted her, she would put her plan into action.

She did not have to wait long the following day. While taking a rest from her run, she sat against the Guardian Oak. Tara gave her the missing pieces she needed.

On the weekend, she found herself sitting next to Rex at the lower end of a long dining table. It had taken Ariana a while to convince Rex that he did not look a prat in a dinner jacket. In fact, she told him he would probably turn a few heads.

Looking around the table, she saw not only Yendo, but the Home Secretary and the Minister for Education. She thought that both were brighter than the PM, but also ideologues with the same views as Clarant.

She had to clasp Rex's hand tightly when they heard conversations drifting down the table about the influx of migrants ruining the culture. Thankfully, he stayed calm. She now realised that it was not just Clarant who was infected by the desires Cernounos had given him. There was a whole group of influential people who shared the same greed and who despised those less privileged than themselves. Monday could not come soon enough. She had made her plans.

~

When Monday did come, Ariana found that she alone had been called to meet Clarant. She felt something was very wrong, but kept her cool.

"I am sending Rex away. I am sorry, Ariana, but I no longer want him here."

"Well, I'm sorry too. You have made a big mistake, for if Rex goes I go with him."

"I thought you would respond this way."

Rex came in, with Colin holding a gun to his back. Ariana laughed.

"So, what do you think this is going to achieve?"

"I can let Rex go if you agree to stay and serve me."

Ariana stared at Clarant.

"Do you know where yesterday is, Clarant? I guess you do, but listen, I wasn't born there! I can read you as easily as I can read Yendo and the rest of them. She reached out and tore away Clarant's memories and talents. Clarant fell to his knees and stayed there looking around with a totally blank face.

"What have you done to him?"

Colin crossed to his stricken master. As he bent to speak to him, Ariana moved in behind him and placed a hand on his head. She tried her best to remove his memories of herself and Rex.

"Come, Rex, it's time to get out of here."

As they walked towards the doors, Colin, in his confusion and anger, raised the gun and fired. Ariana fell. In a fit of anger, Rex crossed the room and tore the gun from Colin's hands; he was about to fire it into Colin's head when Ariana screamed, "No!" He dropped the gun, saying the bastard would have deserved it. Ariana had been hit in the leg and was losing blood.

"Come and help me, Rex. By tomorrow they will have no idea what has happened to them.

Rex headed towards the Deer park and a gap in the fence, carrying Ariana in his arms. A beat-up old VW was waiting just outside to take them to safety.

Chapter 29

"Hospital?"

"No, get me back to the farm. Do what I say to stop the blood. Anna, you drive. Josie, use the wind to put a torque around my leg so you can manage the blood flow. Rex, keep out of the way; they know what they are doing."

Anna drove as fast as she could in a camper van that could never go past 55 miles an hour.

When they arrived at the farm, everyone flew into action. Denfar came with Itana and Itana explained who he was. Ariana knew her from Spain and relaxed as they set to work. She awoke the next day with a worried-looking Rex stood near the doorway.

Meldrum arrived with Denfar and Itana. Denfar spoke up. "I am still learning, Ariana, so I have brought the mistress with me."

"Look, you idiots," said Meldrum, "if you'd left her alone she would have probably worked out how to heal herself. Do we have to rush to help everyone who has a pinhole in their thigh? Now, tell me who this handsome stranger is; better still, let him tell me. Well?"

Rex stared at the old woman.

"I am Rex, friend and colleague of Ariana. We worked together, but now I must admit I am lost. If you want to know me, ask her. Who the hell do I ask to find out who you are?"

There was general laughter, then Narsin turned to face Rex.

"We know you, Rex, but you must be patient. Soon an explanation of who we are, and what you might be, will be given to you. Then you must decide if you want to take the invitation your Talent grants you. A room will be made available for you until you make your choice."

~

Father Gary heard the phone ringing; when he picked it up, he was surprised and relieved to hear Ariana's voice. "You are alive, thank God."

"Yes, Father Gary, it seems I am. Do you need to touch me to make sure?"

"Will you never stop teasing me? I have been going out of my mind with worry."

"Gary, you have faith in your Trinity, but so little in me. We do not need to worry. The spirits are with us in the fight we must pursue. The spirit that gives you strength gives me strength also."

"Sorry, Ariana, that does not stop me thinking of the day they came for you with guns and I was unable to do anything to stop them."

"There was nothing you could have done. Anyway, now I have the knowledge to piece together Clarant's plan. We would not have that if I had not been taken. I think I will take another day's rest then I must talk to the Meldrums about the way forward. I am going to put the phone down now. Ring again soon."

Ariana lay her head back on the pillow and fell into a gentle sleep.

~

Rex was completely at a loss. He sat on a bench outside the meal room. Narsin had called for him early, to take him to first-meal. Immediately afterwards, they went to the cottage, and Rosa explained the history of the Pixsan. They told him to take time and think about what he had been told.

Everybody was about their business, and he had been left to think things through. He was about to get up and walk around when the two women from the van approached him. They stood out from the others as they never wore the Pixsan white. The one called Josie wore a leather jacket and denim jeans torn at the knee; her feet were shod with Doc Martens and her jet black hair was cut in a short bob. Her companion, Anna, wore a woollen cardigan over a short green dress, thick bright red tights and pale yellow ankle boots. Her unruly red hair almost reached her waist.

"So, hero, what happened?"

"I'm not a hero, and I've no idea what she did to those two bastards to stop them in their tracks. I never thought I'd see a grown man like Clarant cry, but whatever she did she brought him to his knees."

"Sounds like she messed with his mind. A powerful woman, our Ariana."

"I guessed she was strong, but I had no idea what she could do."

"Sorry, Rex, you are at the very bottom of a steep learning curve. Anna and me were like you once. When we arrived I had no idea who the Pixsan were, but I would have gone mad if they'd not rescued me and brought us here. What we are saying, Rex, is that if you need someone to talk to who knows what you are going through then seek us out."

"Thank you. Now, can you tell me something? Ariana put herself at risk for me, a guy she hardly knew. I know she could have left at any time. What..."

Josie interrupted him.

"There was something she needed to find out. When she had that information she was ready to leave. I'm sure, given time, she could have removed parts of Clarant's memory and left him functioning, but because he threatened you she had no choice. She had to act quickly, so she tore out his memory and his ability to resist Talent-holders. He'll recover, but our guess is that his physicians will diagnose a stroke which caused memory loss. Ariana did her best to wipe you and herself out of Colin's mind and it's doubtful if he will remember, but we must find out. That's why we want you to come with us to Clarant's. You and Josie will pose as security there to check the newly installed security cameras. I will keep the engine running. There must have been other staff. How did they fit in?"

"There were, but they were all in the other wing of the house. We were kept like prisoners for most of the time. Outside caterers were brought in for the events we attended."

"OK then, Rex, are you up for this?"

"Yes, I can't wait."

Anna laughed, "Neither can I. I can't wait to see Josie looking smart for a change. We will have to wait for the Tort Mae to agree first though."

"Tort Mae?"

"They will appoint someone to teach you the Histories soon. They will tell you what you need to know.

The one sentence you need to remember is – don't ever mess with the Tort Mae."

~

Narsin, Rosa and Meldrum sat with Ariana. Denfar had insisted she stay in bed for a while, so they had come to her.

"This is how I see it," she explained.

She told them Clarant had gained the ear of the Prime Minister's chief adviser, a man called Don Yendo. Yendo was a very bright maverick; he did not care about convention, and despised the state bureaucracy. He would use any method to get his way, legitimate or not. "Clarant had used two methods to win over Yendo. Firstly, he had used Colin to plant ideas into Yendo's head. This was not difficult, as Clarant and Yendo are extreme, free-market, neo-liberals. His aim was to cut regulation, reduce workers' rights and reduce the role of the state even further than the preceding right-wing governments. He wanted as many workers as possible on zero-hour contracts, and state aid to the unemployed and disabled cut to the barest minimum. He knew this might cause social unrest and that it would be hard for a PM who always wanted to be popular to take this on. But Yendo argued that these policies were what the paymasters of his party wanted and he was winning the PM over. Yendo's reward was to be shares in one of Clarant's companies.

"When you sent me the details of his investments, one stood out: the company owned by him that made equipment for the police and the armed forces. Body armour, tasers, water cannon, etc. With widespread civil unrest, he stood to make a lot of money. We know how all this would benefit Cernounos.

"Because I had to act so quickly we have been left with several problems. The first is Colin, Clarant's sidekick. I think I removed most of his memory, but I was rushed and cannot be sure. Secondly, the wound to my leg. I covered it with my sash but there must have been a few drops that escaped. If they find them they will have my DNA. Thirdly, Yendo's minders from MI5 know me. I'm going to have to disappear for a long time which, I might add, is OK by me. That sort of excitement I could do without. They never met Rex, but they may have some photos of him sitting next to me during the final weekend gathering."

Rosa turned to Ariana and asked what she thought they should do next.

"I know the Tort Mae are not going to like what I have to say. The Pixsan have avoided interfering in human affairs for centuries. Now we have no choice. Times are no longer so simple. As I see it, if we do not intervene, Cernounos will win. The Prime Minister is weak. At the moment he is under the influence of Don Yendo who is in turn under the influence of people like Clarant.

"They are extreme ideologues who care little for humanity, but a lot about profit. They are in denial about the threat to the environment and will not listen to the best scientific or spiritual advice. They blame everyone else for things that go wrong: immigrants, environmentalists, the so-called lazy poor who they say keep having too many children. They are terrified of losing their money. They truly have the blood of dragons and will never share their wealth. They must be curtailed or brought to the truth.

"There are other more progressive politicians and a few old guard who think differently and still care about the lives of ordinary people. No matter what follows, we have to turn the PM away from the extreme right-wing ideologues. We have to take Yendo away from a position where he can influence those in power. We will have to be careful: the security services are following Yendo like shadows. Not just the ones I met, but probably MI6 too. We are going to have to plan well to avoid becoming known to them. So far, we are on none of their databases and we must avoid their attention. However, we have been charged with policing Cernounos. We have no choice and we have many allies on our side."

Chapter 30

The Tort Mae had been called and had discussed Ariana's report. She who wore the green stood at the Head of the Place Apart.

"We are about to go out into a world we know little about. Those of our young who have the skill must be moved here. We will create a centre of intelligence to monitor those with Dragon Blood. Those who can must enter society. We will need agents among the Dragon Bloods whose greed threatens the spirits of the earth. The Daughters must be recalled. Leana, the Daughter of Fire, must return to us. We are in the hour of the greatest threat that has ever faced us. We thank the spirits that have sent us Tara, she who brings help from the Dryads. Their paths of communication will prove invaluable. Also Denfar, for we fear that Ariana will not be the last to suffer from the wounds iron weapons bring. We have not forgotten Itana and Rafael. Without them, and those who are to come, our struggle would be greater.

"The war is declared. It will not be announced, but from this day on by fair means or foul we fight to save our world."

The woman in green stepped back, calling for any other business to be raised before the Tort Mae. Rosa stepped forward.

"Sisters, we have a stranger among us. Will you judge his worthiness so that he can become Pixsan? Ariana will stand witness."

All listened as Ariana spoke for Rex. The woman in green called him forward.

"Rex, you have been spoken for. Will you eat the fruit of the companion to the oak?"

Rex was not prepared for this and knew the fruit of the mistletoe to be poisonous, but he did not care. He had only lived for a short time among the Pixsan, but he wanted nothing more than to be one of them. He took the white berries and swallowed them. He heard a multitude of voices in his head but held still.

"Rex, do you accept the authority of the Tort Mae?"

"Yes."

Meldrum stepped forward.

"Rex, if you accept this invitation, your past falls from you. If you change your mind, there will be consequences, but none that will bring you harm. Do you accept the invitation to the House of Meldrum?"

Rex was about to say try and stop me, but instead answered a simple yes.

A welcome came from the voices in his head.

Chapter 31

Tara and Rafael sat in the rooms over the woodshed. Rafael wanted to know what Tara thought would happen next. Meldrum considered she could teach them no more so they would need to go back to working in the community, Rafael at the allotment gardens and Tara wherever she was needed. The Dryad had asked them to go occasionally to the Guardian Oak, but said she would call if Tara was needed urgently. They agreed they would talk to Rosa about it the following day. Tara picked up her bag and they headed off for family-meal.

When they arrived, Tara noticed a newcomer sat at the foot of the table next to Rex. His complexion was dark and his hair the black of the Pixsan, but he lacked the physical calmness the others seemed to have. Engaged in conversation with Rex, he was using his arms to add emphasis to something he was saying. She realised how uncommon it was to see a Pixsan do this; they always appeared so relaxed.

When the meal was over, Narsin stood and welcomed the newcomer, Arwan. He was from Wales and was to be part of a new team which would develop the Pixsan's computer capabilities. The House of Meldrum would no longer be a training centre for the Resistants. Those who had been trained and had shown themselves capable of teaching would set up new regional centres. The farm was to draw together those who would take the lead in the war against the Dragon Bloods.

Arwan was one of the first to answer the call for those with a high level of IT and software knowledge. Others would come to be given the knowledge Ariana and Rex had gained. They would be sent out to infiltrate Dragon Blood circles. The reserves of the Tort Mae would be strained by all this, but they were already looking outwards for more streams of revenue. Now there were Pixsan who could move freely in the world of iron, all sorts of opportunities were going to open up.

Not long after Tara and Rafael had returned to the woodshed, Itana and Denfar turned up with the newcomer Arwan and several bottles of mead wine. Tara, who was hoping for a quiet night, sighed internally. She thought that at least with Arwan present she would not have to put up with Itana's remarks about her and Rafael, but as soon as they arrived, Itana, with a broad smile on her face and mischief in her eyes, asked her how they were getting on. Denfar shrugged and Rafael turned away from the two women.

"Look at him, Tara, he's turned away to hide his blushes."

Tara ignored her and turned to Arwan.

"Welcome, Arwan. I am Tara and this is Rafael. Whereabouts in Wales are you from?"

"I suppose my name gives my origins away. I come from a very small community in the north. We live beyond a lake called Cwm Bychan in the folds of the mountains. I won a scholarship to study maths and computer sciences in Aberystwyth. To be honest, the community was not sure about me going. The farm there is all about livestock and the work is hard, but the Tort Mae promised to send a replacement for me and insisted I go. I'm a Resistant, so I did not mind. Truth is, I loved life at the university. Something about computers and programming suits me. I love numbers and probabilities."

All this, Tara thought, was said at twice the speed of normal Pixsan speech. She could not help but like this enthusiastic Welshman. As the wine flowed, Tara and Arwan fell into close conversation, almost as if the others were not there. Arwan was fascinated by Tara's studies in Oxford and argued that mathematical probabilities were as important when examining the past as they were when looking at possible trends in the future. For Tara, the evening rushed by and soon they were all saying goodnight. As they were leaving, Itana looked into Tara's eyes and nodded toward Rafael. She turned. Oh no, she thought; Rafael looked totally dejected. Itana had been right all along. What on earth was she going to do now.

She had grown comfortable with Rafael's company, almost taken it for granted. She enjoyed it when they worked together. He was undoubtedly attractive, but all this was just too strange. In a matter of months, things had changed so completely for her. She would have to make him try and understand. She would speak to Itana and ask they be left alone the following evening. She would try and explain how she felt. At the moment, she had to master her new self – relationships were just too difficult. She did not want to commit to anything until her new identity had settled.

~

Tara spent the next day dreading the coming of evening. She had asked Rafael before he left for work if he minded them eating at home; she would cook. He nodded his assent, but said nothing more as he headed off to the garden. She had tried to make herself busy, but they did not always have work for her to do. Late in the afternoon, she sought out Itana.

"I did try to warn you last night. Denfar and I tried to distract him – his eyes never left you and Arwan. I could see he was becoming more and more agitated. What is wrong with you, Tara? Let me tell you, I know exactly how he must be feeling right now and it will not be good. I am not sure whether your lack of awareness of what was happening makes your actions more or less forgivable."

"I've been a fool; I didn't mean to be cruel."

"From where I was sitting, you made a fairly good job of it. I thought anthropologists were supposed to understand human behaviour. The fact that Rafael is going to be tied to you and have to work with you every day is going to be agony for him. I know that in theory it shouldn't matter. You could have separate partners, but you are tied in the Talent, and unrequited love in a situation like this is going to make things hard for both of you. You saw what I went through. Thank the spirits I was wrong about Denfar. I am not sure just how you are going to work this out. Buena suerte! ...as they say at home."

Itana walked away, leaving Tara feeling ten times worse.

Evening came and she looked at the mess she had made of cooking a simple meal. She just couldn't focus. When Rafael returned, they both put on a brave face. He went to wash and change and she laid the table. When he reappeared she immediately started apologising about the food. Rafael poured some wine. She took a gulp; it didn't help. He just sat there calmly.

"OK, Tara, this is how I see it."

She started to speak; he asked her to wait until he'd said what he wanted to say.

"I think you have come to realise what is in my heart, Tara; in fact, I know you have. Denfar came to see me in the garden today. At one time I thought him unfortunate, but I am beginning to think he is a very lucky man. It is clear you do not share my feelings, so we will have to work this out in some other way. Tomorrow I will ask for a change of quarters. I could not bear another evening like yesterday's. Working together will not be easy, but I am Pixsan and will do what I must."

"Now, Rafael, you must listen to me and not interrupt. I'm not Pixsan. I was brought up in a different world. A world where magic did not exist and tree spirits were just old tales from the past. Like you, I did not volunteer to come here. Our spirits compelled us. But for me it's different: I am in a whole new world and I have changed. I have hardly adjusted to what I have become and I am full of self doubt about my ability. Your friendship has been a valuable part of my struggle to come to terms with my new identity. I'll be honest, I don't know at this moment if what I feel for you is love. I only know that I will be devastated if you moved out. I know I am asking a lot, maybe the impossible, but please be patient and stay. I admit I have been stupid and last night was the height of my stupidity. Itana has told me just how much. I will not be so unthinking again."

Silence reigned for a while, then Rafael spoke.

"I would not lose your friendship, Tara, so I will stay and help you all I can, but if you find your heart seeks someone else, I must be the first to know."

"Rafael, please listen – until I know myself, I will not know my heart. Please give me time."

They finished the wine and headed for their rooms. Tara swore to herself she would do everything she could never to hurt him again.

Chapter 32

Ariana sat playing chess with Rex. She wanted to know how he was coping with being Pixsan. He explained that he felt he had come home.

"I look around me and I can feel the power in all of you. I always thought you strong, Ariana, but there are others here who are stronger. I want to talk to Meldrum the Elder, but she is always busy."

Ariana smiled.

"You see the power in us, Rex, and that makes you a rare Talent. You are a Talent sensitive, and you will be invaluable in our fight with the Dragon Bloods. When we move among them you will know when they have captured a Wild. I will arrange for you to talk to Meldrum tomorrow. You may need a little training. She loves handsome men, so beware."

Rex laughed, but he knew how strong Meldrum was, and was not without a little fear.

~

After a few weeks, everything seemed to have gone quiet at the farm. Word was that Rosa, Narsin, Josie and Anna had gone to the House of the Mer to meet with Charly and the other Daughters. Leana, Josie's sister, had returned from Spain, and Tessa and Dylan had travelled over from Torrington. The Tort Mae were to gather in two days' time and messages had come to the farm calling for Ariana, Rex, Tara, Rafael and Denfar and Itana to join them. When they arrived, they found the old hotel busy with women they assumed were of the Tort Mae.

Corrin met them and found them rooms. He showed Tara and Rafael to a room with two single beds. "Sorry, you two; things are tight here so you are going to have to share a room." Tara thought better about asking to share a room with Itana. Denfar and Itana were in Declared singles rooms so she knew it could not be.

"Don't worry, Tara, we will muddle through. I have had to share before in the shepherd huts of our mountains. They were places of night refuge, for both women and men, when we were out looking after the sheep. It is just a matter of organising a routine. There is one problem, though: I hope you don't snore."

Rafael ducked as a pillow came flying at him from across the room.

When Tara woke up, Rafael was long gone. She suspected he had gone to the garden in the neighbouring combe. She went to shower and, as usual, found it in the immaculate condition Rafael always left things in. She washed quickly, hoping she would still find food in the meal room.

The lack of clocks or time pieces still confused her. She need not have worried – Itana and Denfar were there among many others waiting for first-meal. Rafael must have been up with the sparrows as he was nowhere to be seen. Tara took some breakfast from the table the old men had lain with food and went and sat next to Denfar and Itana. Itana looked serious when she asked how things were going. Tara told her they were doing as well as they could be. Itana said she was worried about what they were doing to one another. Denfar butted in, telling Itana that they must work things out for themselves.

"Rafael has me, and Tara has you. We will listen and help all we can. Soon there may be no time to think of such things. My guess is that we are heading into a situation the Pixsan have not faced for centuries: we will be going into a clandestine war against the Dragon Bloods, a new breed who care only for themselves. I suspect the reason I am here is that lives are going to be at risk and may be lost."

They all fell silent for a while.

~

The meetings lasted for two days and resulted in plans that would change many of the Pixsan's lives. The core majority, the iron sensitives, would stay at the farms. It was decided that those with the right Talent must relocate to Bristol, where they would set up a centre of operations. From there, Pixsan could act quickly against Cernounos' activities on the city's periphery. Josie and Anna would head up the taskforce and respond as necessary. The centre at the farm would use the new technologies to monitor the Dragon Bloods. To help identify them, several of the key figures would disperse. Tara was to apply to go back to Oxford where the academic expert on Cernounos, Perry Beglott, still held a post.

They had no idea how much Clarant had shared about Talent-holders to the members of the group he had been putting together at Clerkendale.

For those with little knowledge who wanted to know more, it was thought that Perry would be an obvious place to start. Tara and Rafael were to befriend him, discover who made up his social circle and who his academic and research contacts might be.

Tessa and Dylan had gained many friends in the music business and beyond. They were always being invited to celebrity events. So far, the invitations had been turned down. Now they would take advantage of their musical celebrity. The worlds of celebrity, business and politics were closer than most people realised. Country house parties were definitely not Dylan's thing, but they realised their potential for gathering information on the Dragon Bloods.

There was no role for Itana and Denfar at the moment so they were to be relocated to the House of the Mer to help with the Medicine Garden. Charly and Corrin were also to remain and carry on with their project. The sea would eventually allow quick access to other parts of Albion without the discomfort that modern overland travel brought for most of the Pixsan.

With the promise of reforms to come, Rosa had now accepted a key role in the Tort Mae. It had been too cumbersome in the present struggle, and some decisions needed to be made quickly. A smaller group had been set up to deal with the fight against Cernounos. Rosa, Narsin, Leana, Josie and Anna and the Tanners would form this group. Meldrum and Konia would work with the new group at the farm. It would be developing the IT skills they needed for observing and collating the activities of the Dragon Bloods.

Chapter 33

It did not take long for Tara to re-establish her contacts with Oxford. She had worked with Rosa on a research proposal. The project would look at the persistence of ideas and values from folklore, and how and where they appeared in modern day British life. This would give her access to the History Department and Perry Beglott. Her project application was accepted and she found herself with associate status for the course of her research. She needed somewhere to stay outside the college and eventually found a small house to rent on a suburban street.

Tara guessed Rafael was not pleased at the prospect of being in a city. She had found the place when she had first gone back to Oxford after her project had been accepted. The Faculty of Social Anthropology had welcomed it. It was a sound proposal which had the benefit of being funded by an outside source.

The house was unfurnished, so mattresses on floors, then trips to Ikea were needed. It did not take long to get the place habitable. Now she had to deal with Rafael. There was literally nothing for him here. No job, no friends, and only evenings with Tara, which she spent shut away working. Rafael never complained, but she could see he was unhappy. When she had arrived home that evening he had cooked a meal. They had agreed to take it in turns to cook. The truth was, he was a much better cook than her, so he had quickly become the one to deal with the food.

"I am not sure you need me here, Tara."

"Oh, Rafael, the last time I was here they tried to abduct me near the college. I know it's a drag babysitting me; please be patient. Now, I have a favour to ask. I want to invite a couple for dinner on Saturday night. He is an old colleague of mine whose work has mostly been based in Brazil. He has only just found someone. She works in what was once called botany, but is now called plant sciences. I think she has some connections with the arboretum."

Rafael perked up. Like all Pixsan males, he enjoyed cooking and trained from an early age. Someone with a knowledge of trees to talk with over dinner would be good.

"They are not vegan, are they? Not that it matters. I can cook something edible without meat or dairy, but spice is no real replacement of meat juices."

"I will ask, although I guess that most anthropologists eat what they are given as they do not want to upset those they presume to study."

Rafael laughed. "I wonder what they would make of us if they knew the truth?"

"They must never know, Rafael." He nodded in agreement.

~

Rafael was the first to see the guests arrive. The window of the tiny galley kitchen overlooked the small front garden and the road where they parked their car. The guy was tall, smartly dressed in casual clothes and wore a short beard. Rafael wondered if this style, so similar to that of his tutors at the University of Vigo, was the same for academics everywhere. The woman was shorter and wore a green dress over dark green stockings. Her black hair was shoulder length. Rafael guessed that she came from a South-East Asian background. She had obviously made an effort for her partner's old friend.

Tara answered the door and showed them in, apologising all the time for the sparseness of the place. "Can't wait to get some pictures on the walls and some shelves to place my books on," she told them. The smell of spiced meat filled the air. Tara called for Rafael to meet the others, and he appeared from the kitchen explaining the food would soon be ready. "Rafael, this is Kelvin and Anoja. Kelvin, Anoja meet Rafael."

"Good evening, Tara, and boa tarde, Rafael."

Rafael smiled. Of course Kelvin would speak Portuguese as he had worked in Brazil, and Galician and Portuguese were similar. Tara looked a little puzzled and turned towards Rafael who replied to Kelvin with the greeting, "Muito prazer."

"That's enough, you two. Let's keep to a language we can all understand."

"Si Senhora, Tara," the two men said in unison. The evening passed pleasantly, with Tara trying not to appear too engaged in her conversation with Kelvin. She noticed that Rafael was not quite so circumspect as he and Anoja discussed their common objects of study.

They both appeared animated when talking about a visit to the arboretum. This did not pass Kelvin's notice. Kelvin had asked Tara if they were a couple. Not knowing quite what to say, she had quickly replied that they were just housemates. Now she could see a spark of jealousy in Kelvin's eyes.

Time to send them home, she thought. The evening ended with a promise to Rafael from Anoja to show him around her department and the arboretum. Kelvin thanked them both for a lovely evening.

After seeing them out, Tara and Rafael returned to the sitting-room.

"I think you made Kelvin a little green there, Rafael."

"I am undeclared, Tara. Are your friends declared? She is an interesting woman and very intelligent; why should I not engage with her?"

Tara looked at him and uttered one word.

"Arwan."

"OK, if I made your friend feel uncomfortable, I apologise."

"I am afraid it was not just Kelvin you made uncomfortable."

"What are you saying, Tara?"

Tara tried to put her thoughts together. What had she felt when she had seen Rafael and Anoja so easy in each other's company? It was like wanting someone, but not knowing why. She could not easily remove the barriers she had so carefully made for herself. In her determination to do well as an academic, she had pushed aside any possibility of becoming romantically entangled with someone. She carefully analysed those around her, wondering how they held their relationships together, and when some relationships fell apart she tried to work out what had gone wrong for them. She was attractive and men were drawn to her, but she had the habit of over-analysing what a relationship with them would be like. Sometimes this happened before they even got through their first date. As a result, it never got much further than that. She had male friends with whom she shared an intellectual interest, but they were just colleagues.

She was often invited to dinner parties by them and their wives. The wives would always invite a single male when their husbands announced she was coming. Their seating plans always put her beside them. Feeling she had been set up, she never really engaged with any of them.

Now she was in a different world, the world of the Pixsan and in front of her was a man she found attractive and who thought he loved her. His patience confused her. His gentleness unsettled her. They had little in common but maybe that was it. They needed to know more about each other, or at least she needed to know more about him. She walked across to the sofa and sat down.

"Tell me about where you grew up, Rafael."

Rafael did not push his question further. He stood, poured the remaining wine into two glasses then returned to sit beside her.

Chapter 34

The following day, Tara rang the History Department. She asked if she could speak to Perry Beglott, but was told by a secretary that he did not accept calls. However, if she sent him an email giving the reasons she wished to contact him he may respond.

The tone of her voice suggested that Tara should not hold out much hope. Nevertheless, she carefully crafted a letter explaining her research and showed it to Rafael, to see what he thought. He suggested a few changes and she sent it off to Beglott. If he did not answer, they would have to find another approach. Two weeks went by before a reply eventually came.

Perry explained that his research was now concerned with the Anglo Saxon period of British History and he had not added anything to his earlier research on pre-Celtic folklore for several years. He had been surprised by recent interest in his early work and especially his work on Cernounos, the mythical Spirit of Renewal. Tara and Rafael worked together on a carefully worded reply.

They did not mention Cernounos, but emphasised that Perry's knowledge of early folklore would help her develop her project. Could she bring her research assistant with her and could he take notes during their meeting? It was six days before she had a reply to her email. He apologised, explaining that he suffered from debilitating headaches. He didn't know why; they seemed to come whenever he returned to his early research.

It was another four weeks before they actually had a meeting arranged. It was to be in his rooms in the Faculty.

That evening, they sat together on the sofa. They had grown closer over the past weeks, but something was stopping them taking their relationship further. With a slight blush to her cheeks, Tara asked how the Pixsan viewed relationships and how they educated their young about sex.

"These are complicated issues, Tara. You know about the Caution but a lot happens before then. Our young are educated about their bodies from a very early age. When puberty arrives, boys and girls are taken aside by their birth mothers who explain what is happening to them. Teenage years are just as fraught as in your own society.

"Experimenting is neither encouraged nor frowned upon. Jealousy and envy are dealt with openly. If a boy or girl is rejected, there is a tendency for bitterness to develop which, if not checked, can lead to tragedy. Girls are encouraged to form groups to befriend a rejected boy and boys to befriend girls. This way, rejection is less painful and the odd cruel remark from the unthinking can be ignored.

"These friendships can be quite profound and last many years. The Caution exists for those who want to spend the rest of their lives together, though even this is not binding. On rare occasions, those who have grown apart go before the Tort Mae. They then serve a sort of reverse caution. If after the time given them by the Tort Mae they still wish to separate they simply walk away from each other. As property is held in common and children are raised by the whole community, we do not see the problems your society faces when people separate."

"Have you no stroppy teenagers?"

"What you must realise, Tara, is the fact that almost every Pixsan is strongly linked to the land. The knowledge that moving from the community out into the world of forged iron breaks that link is enough for the majority to conform. Some do need to experience it and they are taken to a city by those of us who are not Sensitives. They find it so alien, and the breaking of their link so uncomfortable that they never want to repeat the experience.

"There are some whose link is very weak and want adventure. We explain that their memories of their community will be removed. If they insist, we remove all thoughts of the Pixsan world from their minds and send them to families in the city who we pay to watch out for them. When they grow older, they are on their own. Sometimes we hear they are suffering, and then we send someone to talk to them. If it is judged that they might contribute to their community, they are returned and their memories are restored."

"That seems rather harsh, Rafael."

"When your people have been persecuted for centuries, you will do everything you can to protect them. We never really abandon anyone, but we cannot take risks, especially now, when exposure and capture might turn us into lab rats for the Dragon Bloods."

"Did the women at the farm support you? I am sure Itana told them all that I had treated you badly."

"I think you do Itana a disservice. She is a true friend to us. Anyway, none of the women would help me as they knew I had become your amplifier and that if we could not Caution we would have to become friends."

Tara found herself blushing again as she asked Rafael if he'd had many lovers.

He laughed. "Have you not been listening, Tara?"

"I have, but it is so very different from the world I grew up in."

"And you, Tara, have you had many lovers?"

"None."

Rafael smiled disbelievingly.

"No, take me seriously, Rafael. I grew up as an only child closely protected by my parents, closeted and constantly pushed to achieve. They were proud of me when I entered Oxford and I was happy to have pleased them. I guess in my seriousness to become successful I kept away from anyone who might distract me from my work. So, yes – I am twenty-eight, too busy before, but now I have you in front of me."

"I see. So can we go to bed now?"

"We could, you swine, but I have no desire for motherhood just yet."

"Our women discovered how to control their fertility long ago. Come, I have some of what we need."

Chapter 35

The meeting at Beglott's rooms was a curious affair. They were taken there by a departmental secretary who made it plain how lucky they were to gain an interview. His study was on the sixth floor, and doubled as a seminar room for those who chose to study under him. The smell of linseed oil from recently treated oak doors hung in the air. It reminded Tara of Sundays spent in church when she was a young girl.

Perry invited them to sit in the two seats placed before his desk, but did not stand to greet them or offer to shake hands. All the walls were floor to ceiling with books. Some were a surprise. Tara spotted several early Marvel comics and when she asked about them he explained that old folk tales went through many changes. Over the centuries they often turned up in the most surprising places.

"Take dragons," he said, "nobody has seen one, but everyone will tell you what they are supposed to look like. There are lots of things that lurk in our minds that are part of some ancient folk knowledge."

"How far did your research take you into pre-iron age lore?"

"Not far. When I look back at my early papers it seems to me that I was obsessed with the earth spirit Cernounos. Perhaps that is what led to my breakdown, my obsession, I mean. I left all that work behind me long ago, so it strikes me as odd that someone like Gregory Clarant is writing asking for an interview. Even more odd was a phone call yesterday from one of the Prime

Minister's advisers asking if I had written any work of interest on the subject that remained unpublished. You have not come to ask about Cernounos have you?"

Tara smiled. "No, Perry – if I may call you that?"

"Please do."

"Thank you. My interest and that of my co-researcher, Rafael, is purely in the transfer of folk lore through the ages."

"Ah yes, I see; well, most of my time nowadays is taken up with the research and teaching of our Anglo Saxon period, but I have done some research in the area you talk of. I have no intention of publishing it, and would be happy to share my notes with you. I will send copies to your department. Unfortunately, they are many and quite chaotic!"

"Thank you, Perry; we are very grateful. This is incredibly generous on your part."

"I only ask that if you publish you will give full credit to any of my research which you use."

"That goes without saying. Now, would it be appropriate for us to call on you as we progress? Your insights into any manuscript prior to publication would be invaluable to us."

"Yes, thank you. I did look up the paper you wrote alongside the archaeology group's work on the Dartmoor hut circle. Impressive! I will be glad to help."

~

Back at the house, they opened their last bottle of mead wine.

"Well, Tara, that was an interesting manipulation of the truth you wove for Perry. I wonder if the same process was taking place last night when you told me you loved me?" The cushion hit him square this time.

"When we decide to Declare, then you might find out. In the meantime, I find Perry quite an interesting fellow. The Pixsan may have saved him from Cernounos but he has persevered with his academic career. He has written some really insightful books and I can't wait to read his notes."

This time the cushion flew from Rafael's hands.

In the morning, they would send news to the farm that Yendo was becoming interested in the work that Clarant had begun.

Chapter 36

The Tech centre at the farm had grown too quickly, and Rosa and Narsin were concerned that it would draw attention. Lots of thought had gone into its development, and they had set up their own data storage facilities to avoid the large corporate ones. However, large amounts of electricity was needed to run the computer centre, and this was going to be noticed.

The presence of so many new people was upsetting the balance at the farm. After discussing this with the Tort Mae, it was decided that the computer centre would move to Bristol and be combined with the Response team in a new location. The old Refuge would reopen, but with someone new that Father Gary would recommend, a fellow priest with no knowledge of the Talented. They needed the Refuge to be a dead end, a well-intentioned Christian refuge, but nothing more.

The new base for the united Tech and Response teams was to be on an anonymous trading estate in south Bristol. Arwan had turned out to be a brilliant organiser, both intellectually and practically and, much to the relief of Rosa, he took charge of the move. Rosa was looking forward to visiting the new centre and catching up with them all.

Meanwhile, Josie and Anna had discussed their plan concerning Clarant with Rosa and Meldrum. They explained that Rex was willing to act as a guide as he knew his way around the grounds. Rosa had doubts and asked Konia and Meldrum to look for any news or recent references to Clerkendale Manor in the local and national press. There was not much to be found, but they did turn up an interesting article about Clarant in the financial pages of the Telegraph.

The report mentioned a recent illness and the return of Clarant's brother to help out at the estate while Gregory was indisposed. There was some concern about Clarant's absence from the boards of his companies, although the author seemed quite confident his recovery would be swift. Arwan's team was asked to keep an eye open for any references to Clarant they might come across in Government reports. Rosa felt they should wait a few weeks to see what Arwan's team might come up with.

For the fist time in ages, Rosa was beginning to relax. With the students gone and Arwan's Tech team moving to Bristol, the farm had become the quiet place it used to be.

~

Leana was back from Spain, but had elected to stay at the House of the Mer. She was distantly related to Itana and was keen to see how she was. She was surprised to find her in Caution with Denfar. There was no way she would have imagined her with a guy like him. He was quiet, softly spoken and thoughtful. Not entirely, but almost the opposite of Itana. He was also big and towered over her.

They had all found work in the medicine garden while waiting for things to develop. Its mixture of aromas from the herbs and flowers made the garden a relaxing place to work. Denfar took time to explain the medicinal properties of each plant. He was patient and would repeat his answers when Leana found them difficult to remember. She could see why Itana seemed so deeply enthralled by him, although Itana, being Itana, would deny any such thing.

~

Rosa enjoyed the new peace at the farm and several weeks passed during which Rosa and Narsin found more time to share with each other. Things changed when news came from Bristol. The Tech team had managed to hack into the phones of several of the people Ariana had analysed for Clarant. It was clear that Clarant was bringing together a powerful group of bankers, industrialists and politicians. Their texts and emails showed the group had begun to disperse and lose interest after Clarant's collapse.

Initially, there had been much speculation about Clarant's sudden illness. A fastidious, non-smoking, abstemious character like him did not seem the obvious candidate for a stroke; it was reasoned that it could happen to anyone.

Much more mysterious were the emails concerning Colin. He seemed deeply affected by Clarant's illness. He insisted he had a power that allowed him to influence people. That he and Clarant could call on people with extraordinary abilities. The core group dismissed this, but the maverick Don Yendo was interested and had insisted on talking to Colin. Colin was taken to London where the Tech team's trail went cold. The item in the report which worried Rosa most was Colin repeating the name Ariana. The woman, he claimed, had something to do with Clarant's sudden illness.

Emails from Clarant's brother to his mother in the South of France complained about the presence of some of Yendo's minders at the Manor. They seemed to have Government authorisation straight from the PM to examine the place where Clarant had taken suddenly ill and to go through all his papers and computers.

A new plan was taking shape in Rosa's mind, and to carry it out she would need to speak to Josie and Anna.

She left for Bristol the next day with Ariana, Rex, Narsin and Leana.

Chapter 37

The building looked like any of the other industrial offices and warehouses on South Liberty Lane. The sign on the front of the building was small; if you got close enough you could read the words 'Earth Group Research'. There was a telephone number and an email address, both of which were only monitored occasionally.

The entrance to the building led into a small lobby overlooked by four cameras linked to two separate monitors. Metal detectors set off alarms and locked all the doors until thermal images could be examined. The whole building had similar security around the perimeter. Much had been learnt since the kidnap of Ariana. In this building were many of the finest of the Pixsan young Resistants. Only a few of them were gifted with significant Talents, but all were extremely bright.

They had made the place secure themselves, using and adapting cheap and readily available electronic devices. They were a dedicated group; the presence of the Response team helped give them the feeling that they were at the very centre of the fight.

Rex drove Rosa's car into the car park at the front of the building. They all got out and stretched their legs before walking across to the entrance. As they approached the door, a speaker announced its welcome, and the opaque glass doors opened to reveal Josie and Anna waiting with Arwan just inside the lobby.

"How did you manage to put all this together so soon?"

"Rosa, these kids are amazing. They have the Pixsan ethic. They are really focused; they work together without competing or complaining. They know we have to win."

Beyond the offices was a large open space divided into work areas and a dormitory. Those who worked there decided that sleep was only necessary when they needed it, so they had a place where they came and crashed out when they were too tired to work.

The Response team had built their own quarters at the rear of the building. Their needs were different. Josie and Anna had recruited those whose Talent might be useful. All were women, apart from one lad who had come from a Welsh community and shared Corrin's Talent with birds. The women had Talents with fire, earth, air and water, but none were as strong as the Daughters. Their mission required them to be as fit as possible and, as running the streets made them too conspicuous, they had set up a makeshift gym. Rosa and Narsin were impressed.

Straight after they had been shown around, Rosa suggested they discuss what was to be done. They gathered all those needed in the meal room. Before they travelled to Bristol, Rosa and Narsin shared their plan with Ariana and Rex.

At the moment, it was just an outline and could change, though the aim would be the same. It was going to be dangerous, but everyone would be in danger if Cernounos was not dealt with.

Ariana and Rex were to return to Clerkendale, ostensibly to ask how Clarant was doing. They would contact his brother, Jonathan, to arrange an appointment. They were pretty sure he would have instructions to contact Yendo or Carney straight away.

Arwan had set up a comprehensive computer file on Clarant, and managed to hack Clarant's computer before Yendo and his operatives could crack the passwords and codes. They were surprised to find nothing on Cernounos, or Ariana and the other Talents. For Clarant, it must have been his deepest secret, something he never even committed to a computer file. He may have written notes and these may now be in the possession of Yendo. It was a chance they would take.

They would need someone inside the grounds while Ariana was there. Tara would be called and she would enter the Strange to observe the house. She would need to talk to the Dryads to see if they could defend her while she stayed there for a prolonged period. Leana would be near the perimeter ready to use her Talent to create a diversion. Josie and Anna would enter the grounds at the weakest point; if things turned bad, they would intervene. Denfar and Itana would be located nearby in case of injuries inflicted by iron weapons.

"Okay," said Anna, "it's obvious this is turning into a major operation, so what is the objective?"

"We are going to kidnap Yendo."

"You can't be fucking serious. He is right at the heart of Government."

"Yes, he is, but the Government he is at the centre of is corrupt to the core. He is also the backbone the Government does not have. Let's see how they manage without him? We will be against their finest; we must not underestimate them. Our advantage is that they know nothing of what we are. Let us be careful not to show them, but best them nonetheless."

"What is your role in this, Rosa?"

"I will be on hand should my strength be needed and, once we have Yendo tied in Josie's van, I will moderate his consciousness and keep him confused and too weak to act."

"Where will we take him?"

"He must go to the House of the Mer. Charly can examine him and see if his character and obsessions are the result of a conflict which Charly and the Mer can deal with. If not, we will have to return him, although I doubt this will be necessary. Ariana thinks he may be a Latent, but this we don't know."

Josie wanted to know when it would start, and Rosa told her soon. They would return to the farm for now. They needed Arwan's team to find out what they could about Jonathan Clarant. They were counting on him informing Yendo, but they knew he was very different from his brother. A bit of a hippie, Gregory had called him. He might be the type to resist helping Yendo and the guys from Government security. They did not want this: they needed him to entice Yendo to Clerkendale.

~

Rosa wasn't surprised by a request from Leana: she had asked if she could stay and help with the Response team training. She thought that the girls with a limited fire Talent could benefit from her assistance. The whole place had a buzz of excitement about it, and this seemed to play some part in Leana's request. There was little doubt she would be an asset in training the women, so Rosa readily agreed.

The others were a little pleased; at least the car wouldn't be so cramped on the return journey. Then Josie suggested that Gerrant, the avian Talent would benefit from a few weeks in the company of Corrin. Rosa knew this was a good idea, so the others would just have to put up with it.

Chapter 38

Tara was becoming genuinely interested in the project they had set up in Oxford. Perry's notes were very insightful. He had concentrated on tracing every fragment of a few legendary tales right through to the present day. Rafael had also become interested.

"It is sad that he became a servant of the enemy."

"He has recovered from that. I think Meldrum put a barrier in his mind, but, as you can see, his intellectual ability has not been impaired."

Tara felt her phone vibrate and opened it to look at the series of symbols she knew was a code from the farm. Rafael dialled the farm's number from his old Pay-As-You-Go phone. No one answered his call. A text with the Pixsan word for home appeared a few seconds later.

"Well, it looks like we will have to go back soon. This puts a bit of pressure on us, Tara. We are not Declared, so we will not get quarters together. Here we can be lovers; when we return we will have to take what quarters are available."

"Tell me, Rafael, and be totally honest, what do you want us to do?"

"Tara, I have followed a long path to find you. I cannot escape the irony that when I was sent by my Water spirit to find you, I resisted in every way I could. How was I to know what the woman I was sent to find would be like. The Water spirit said I should obey her completely. This may sound mad to one from your culture, but I think that my spirit guide knew what I could not and now, for me, we are already one."

Tara looked right into Rafael's eyes.

"You were very serious there for a moment," said a grinning Tara. "Now let's go to bed and we'll Declare as soon as we get back to the farm. I think on this issue you need to obey me, without question."

~

On the way back, Tara and Rafael planned to give no clues to Itana of their intention to declare. When they arrived, they were surprised that their old quarters were still available. They moved what little they had brought back with them up into the rooms over the woodshed. Denfar and Itana had arrived from the House of the Mer and were now out of Caution. They were sharing a cottage at the old Refuge. The place seemed very quiet. With no students or members of the Tech team, the place had returned to a rural peace.

Tara and Rafael arranged to meet Denfar and Itana at their cottage. Just as they were leaving family-meal, Meldrum asked to speak to Tara, so Rafael went on alone. Meldrum wanted to know if she had contacted the Dryads while she was in Oxford. Tara admitted that she had not. Meldrum told her to go to the Guardian Oak the next day. Dryads, like all elemental creatures, did not like to be neglected. She must retain frequent contact. Agreeing, Tara said she would go to the Guardian first thing.

"So, you and Rafael, Tara?"

"Oh, Meldrum, can you keep a secret?"

"Absolutely not; this is Meldrum you are talking to, but if you must play your games I will tell Itana nothing."

Tara stood up and kissed Meldrum on the head, saying thank you.

"Go away, girl," was Meldrum's only response. She complained to herself that she was becoming too much like a friendly old granny to all these wild waifs and strays. She would have to get her old reputation back.

When Tara arrived at the door to the cottage she could hear laughter from inside. She entered, and Rafael turned to look at her with a sullen face. From the sudden change in Rafael's mood, Itana guessed that nothing had changed between them. The evening went well enough, with Tara and Rafael sitting as far away from each other as possible. Tara left early, claiming tiredness, but Rafael stayed on for a while, talking to Denfar about the progress at the Medicine Garden.

The next day, Tara and Rafael went early to the Guardian Oak. If the Dryads resented her absence they did not show it. As they walked the Strange, she asked the Guardian if the Dryads could or would be willing to protect her if she should need to enter Clerkendale Manor's gardens. She explained what the Pixsan needed to do and why. The Guardian never gave an answer, but asked her to return the next day.

When she came out of the Strange, Tara found Rafael staring down at her.

"Orita came when you were gone. Rosa and Narsin want to see us in their cottage."

Tara stood up and brushed the grass from her white trousers. She wondered at the fact that nothing seemed to stick to Pixsan clothing. Rafael held out a hand. Tara shook her head and he quickly withdrew it.

Rosa wanted a detailed account of their meeting with Perry Beglott. Tara told of attempts to contact him, firstly through Clarant then through Yendo, and how he had been genuine with his sharing of his early research with them. She expressed a desire to follow the research through. Rosa explained that she had already consulted the Tort Mae.

"For the next few years it is going to be important for us to have a contact in a major university like Oxford, someone who can monitor all the research taking place which might impinge on the Pixsan. Computer technology can pull facts together more quickly than the human mind. As a published researcher in the field, you would become aware of all the anthropological and historical work taking place that might lead down obscure paths towards us. We need someone who has the ability to see this coming. Meldrum tells me you need to be staying near a Dryad woodland. There must be several in the Oxfordshire countryside not far from the city itself. We will look into it. Meldrum also told me something else. Would you like to explain? Don't worry, Meldrum is quite good at keeping secrets, no matter what she tells you. Meldrum guessed, but you tell me."

"We were hoping to keep it a secret until you announce it at family-meal tonight. Itana gave Rafael a hard time so we thought we might take her by surprise."

"I will agree to this, but only if you have her as your Caution and you, Tara, move back in with me and Narsin this evening."

"You Pixsan are hard on lovers." said a smiling Tara.

"Tradition, Tara. I am told that many a young girl and boy have been saved from youthful mistakes by the Caution."

That evening at family-meal, a surly-looking Rafael sat next to Tara, who seemed to be ignoring him and intent on talking to Denfar. Itana tried to join in, but Tara would not let her get a word in, and Itana was beginning to get really annoyed. Itana tried to attract Rafael's attention, but he had started talking to the woman next to him. She could see Denfar was just trying to be polite to Tara, although Tara seemed unaware of this and, if she was, did not seem to care. She just kept on talking to him in a way that Itana thought was deliberately designed to exclude her. By the time the meal ended, there was a good deal of tension in the air between the two women. Itana was glad when it was over. She just wanted to talk to Denfar and ask him what on earth was the matter with Tara.

Before she could leave, Narsin stood up from his chair at the head of the table. He called for quiet and asked that everyone remain seated. Looking down the table, his eyes stopped at Itana.

"Itana of the House of Malarta, it is the duty of every Pixsan, when called, to act as a Caution. This duty is asked of you. Do you accept?"

Confused, Itana looked around before answering, "I accept."

"Rafael has declared to Tara and Tara to Rafael; you are to be their Caution."

It seemed that Meldrum was not so good at keeping secrets after all. Cheers of approval went up from those assembled, while Itana looked on, feeling really embarrassed. Denfar held her close and whispered,

"Never mind, my dear – just think of all the fun you can have being their Caution."

"There is that," she said, as she turned to hug a smiling Tara.

Smiling back, she told her, "Oh dear, how you must hate me for being right all along."

Laughing, the two men clasped hands, with Denfar assuring Rafael that the time in Caution would fly by.

Chapter 39

The atmosphere in the meal room suddenly changed when a peregrine falcon flew through the window at great speed. It landed abruptly on the table in front of Meldrum. Meldrum took the cloth hood which hung from its trailing leash and carefully placed it over the falcon's head. The bird seemed relieved to be blind to the chattering crowd around him. Meldrum took a small cannister from where it was tied to its leg and pulled out the note from within. When she looked up from it there was a look of urgency on her face.

"Narsin and Rosa, we must go to the House of the Mer! Charly's waters have broken. The child comes. It is already dusk; we must hurry. Tara, Rafael, Itana and Denfar, you need to be there too. You must ride; tell the girls to fetch the horses. Narsin, you go with them. Rosa, you must take me in that rust heap of yours as near to the House as you can. I will just have to bear the discomfort. All of you ride like the wind. There may be little time."

~

Tara was afraid. They had told her the horse she was riding would not let her fall, and she had seen how they were trained, but Narsin was pushing them hard. No one knew the moor as well as Narsin, and he was leading them by the most direct route he could. The horses galloped after him and jumped low hedges, only pulling up to let Narsin open the gates between the high stone walls. They rode fast towards the coast and soon reached the place on the moor where it began to drop towards the high sea cliffs. When they came to the half hidden lane down to the House, they could see the car parked behind the curve at its top.

Meldrum climbed onto the back of the trailing horse and Narsin pulled Rosa up to sit in front of him. The woodland was alive with the sound of birds and animals. When they passed the rookery, the rooks went wild. The woman from the Medicine Garden came to meet them.

"You are here now, and it may be some time yet. Those on stable duty will take your horses when you reach the House. No need to worry."

Meldrum turned towards her.

"Wise words, my dear. Rosa has done her best to shatter my bones rushing me here but let's be calm. On this night, Corrin is the one we must allow to fret, and fret he will."

The birth of a child to the Pixsan was a communal affair, for the child is not just born to the birth parents, it is born to the whole community. They found Charly in the meal room, surrounded by everyone over the age of sixteen. She lay on a makeshift bed covered in a white sheet. Her face was covered in sweat. She made no sound as she pushed the baby from inside her. A primeval wailing came from the shoreline, unnerving Tara. Rosa told her not to be afraid for it was only the Mer. They were calling to the child. Meldrum moved forward and stood beside Charly. Charly reached out and clasped Meldrum's hand.

"He comes."

The sound from the woods reached a crescendo, as if the child was being born to the creatures as their own.

The Mer had gathered from near and far for the coming of the boy and the sea was full of dark shapes.

Meldrum pulled back the sheet from Charly's knees and lifted the child while Rosa cut and tied the cord that had nurtured him until that moment. A cry of joy went up among those gathered and then everything fell completely silent. In the quiet that followed, hooves could be heard crossing the courtyard.

The antlered head of a huge stag appeared through the wide doorway. Charly kissed the head of the child and gave it into Corrin's hands. He crossed the room and lifted the child towards the head of the stag. The child reached out as if wanting to embrace it. The stag lowered its head until the child could just touch it. Then abruptly it turned, bellowing loudly, and disappeared into the woods.

There was a stunned silence in the room. Meldrum was at a loss. What had she helped bring into the world! When she held the child she could smell the sea and hear the high winds.

"What are we to call the child?"

Corrin looked fondly down at Charly and his newborn son.

"He has told us his name will be Owyn."

"He?"

"Herne, did you not hear?"

"Then his name will be Owyn"

Glasses were raised and Owyn was welcomed to the world.

Charly was carried off on her makeshift bed to their rooms in the old hotel. The families remained and more mead wine was brought to celebrate the new arrival.

The group from the farm sat together discussing the evening's events. Tara was quite confused. She was told that, no, Herne – the spirit of the woods – did not attend every birth, neither did the animal kingdom make such a noise. Charly was close to the Mer. It seemed the others thought that this was all she needed to know, but it was not. Itana and Denfar had been called in case of difficulty, but why had she been called?

Meldrum, who had talked to Corrin before he left to join Charly and Owyn, told her she was to attend Charly and Owyn in the morning. Things were coming to a close and Rafael headed off with the others to his quarters in the hotel. Tara was led away by a young girl whose room she was to share.

~

The next thing Rafael knew was feeling someone shaking him awake.

"Tara! What are you doing? You know..."

"Oh, shut up and get dressed. Do you think I can't be without you for five minutes? The Dryads are calling us to the woods. Quickly, we must go right now."

Rafael dressed as fast as he could, for his head was still clouded with sleep.

"Quickly, man."

"OK, OK, I'm coming.

They crept out of the house and headed up the lane towards the woods. As they left the old hotel, an owl swept down from the eaves and flew up the lane to perch where it could see them. Too tired to ask questions, Rafael just fell in behind Tara, who was rushing ahead of him. When she neared the top, she turned onto a side path which led back down the hillside through thick trees into a moonlit clearing. Before them was the giant stag, with Durantia at his side. Despite the cold of the night air, she wore only a green shift of almost translucent material. From her shoulders sprouted antlers which were a match for Herne's. Tara sank to her knees and Rafael followed suit. Soft words came into their heads.

"Sister of the Dryads, you have been called to serve Owyn. When he is able and wishes it, he will tell you what he needs. Be near to him and grow with him. He is the key to all our futures. Ask no questions, just treat him like all Pixsan will treat him, like a child of your own."

With this, Durantia turned and walked with Herne into the woodland.

They knelt there silent for a while, then Tara said they should get back. As they walked down the lane, she asked Rafael how they were going to explain what had happened. A voice came from the woods, making them both jump.

"I wouldn't worry about that."

They turned to see Corrin sat with his back to an old elm. An owl was perched on the branch above him.

"Owls are very attentive birds and everything this one sees, I see. Now, come and tell Charly everything that's happened. She is awake feeding our child."

Chapter 40

When they got back to the farm, Rosa found a message from Arwan marked urgent. It asked if they had heard the news about Yendo. Rosa and Narsin headed straight round to Konia and Meldrum's rooms. Konia pointed to the computer monitor. There was a headline: 'PM's closest advisor sacked and told to remove his things from his Downing Street office.'

"What does this mean for your plan, Rosa?"

"I think we will still have to deal with Yendo. We don't know why he has been sacked; we do know he still has Colin. This will give him more time to pursue us. We are just going to have to work hard to find out what his next move will be. In the meantime, I think we should go ahead and arrange for Ariana to visit Clerkendale.

"We need to know how Jonathan Clarant will react and if he will contact James Carney. I don't think Carney will let go until he is certain as to what happened with Gregory. He will have heard Colin's claims about Ariana. Perhaps it will be best if we rent a holiday cottage nearby. I think Narsin and I should go with Ariana and Rex. Josie thinks highly of one of their trainees. Apparently she is highly skilled with the wind and has even demonstrated to Josie how she could unlock doors by manipulating a force of air within a lock. We could take her as back-up."

Meldrum the Elder agreed. They drafted a letter with Ariana and Rex and sent it to Clerkendale. The response came by return. Jonathan would be pleased to meet Ariana and Rex. Perhaps they could talk to Gregory and it might stimulate him. It appeared that he did little other than sit in his chair and stare out at the grounds.

Ariana had always felt a little bad about how she had left Gregory. Maybe, if it could be done, she could reverse the worse areas of damage and leave him with some memories of his life before Cernounos. He was an objectionable character, but it was Cernounos who was the source of his most recent corruption.

They rented an old farmhouse near the village of Hawkbridge close to the Clerkendale estate. The house had a garden at the front, planted in the cottage garden manner, with a mixture of flowers and veg. There was even a trellis porch with climbing roses trailing over it. Rosa thought it would have been a nice place for her and Narsin to take a break. They arrived on a bright late spring afternoon and pulled the car into the drive next to the house. Sat outside the kitchen door they found a young woman in a green short-sleeve top, light blue jeans and trainers. Her black curls reached way down her back. She turned to acknowledge them and picked up her large rucksack.

"Hi, we weren't introduced at Earth Research. I am Cormbrenna, but call me Bren; everyone does."

Rosa held out her hand and bowed from the waist then watched as the others did the same.

"Right, let's see what we have inside."

The keys had been left under a tile on top of the water butt. Rosa soon found them and opened the door. The old farmhouse was quite big, with six bedrooms, three of which were ensuite. They chose their rooms, unpacked and headed for the kitchen.

Rex had elected to sleep in the small downstairs bedroom. Here, he explained, he could guard against night-time intruders. Even though he and Ariana were not romantically entangled, Rosa could see that Rex was devoted to her and would do anything to protect her. She smiled to herself, thinking that it would probably be Ariana who would do the saving, if any saving were needed.

After unpacking, they gathered in the large kitchen-diner. Rex busied himself making lamb and field-bean stew from the supplies they had brought from the farm.

Narsin took some mead wine from the fridge while Rosa checked the cupboards for wine glasses. They did not finish eating until late and Rosa, tired from travelling and the effects of the wine, suggested to Narsin they retire. Ariana excused herself and left Rex talking to Bren in the kitchen.

The next morning, Ariana, Bren and Rex were sat at the table when Rosa and Narsin returned from their run.

"What is for first-meal?"

Rex looked a bit glum and sighed before answering. "Stale bread and that fish paste the Mer House lumbers us with in exchange for mead wine."

"Do not complain, Rex," said a smiling Bren "It is not the Pixsan way and, anyway, fish oil is very good for you."

"You obviously don't get enough of it at Earth Research."

"OK, Rex, I think there is some honey in the car."

Rex got up to leave, but stopped as he passed the window facing the road.

"Visitors, Rosa."

Rosa and Ariana crossed to the window.

"Two of them are armed. It seems to be just Carney approaching. Bren, come out the back with me and Narsin. Rex, stay with Ariana; he will expect to find you here."

Carney left the two men by the car and walked slowly up the drive. He was dressed casually in jeans, a white open-neck shirt and a suit coat. On his feet he wore practical black leather shoes. There was no wasted fat on him. He was fit and muscular. He looked around carefully as he approached the door. Before he got there, it opened and a smiling Ariana stood in the doorway.

"We meet again, Mr Carney. I am afraid you have missed breakfast, but do come in."

Carney looked back at his men, indicating for them to wait.

Ariana led him in and they sat in the small-sitting room next to the kitchen.

"How is Clarant?"

"Unwell, Ariana, but you and I both know his illness was not caused by a stroke."

"Then what? Sorry, may I call you James?" He nodded and she continued. "What do you think caused his condition, James?"

"There was a man in my custody. I believe you know him; his name is Colin. He is convinced you caused Clarant's sudden illness."

"And you believe him?"

"What are you, Ariana?"

"Oh dear, you must have worked out that I am female."

Rex grinned and Carney continued.

"I don't think that is hard. No man could mistake you for anything else. Colin says you have some sort of special talent."

Ariana remained silent for a while before answering.

"I see, now let me tell you something about you, Mr Carney. You serve the Crown first and above any politician. You believe in public service. You despise politicians who are only in politics for personal gain. You hate corruption, and the fact that you can do little about it eats away at you. You are a good man, James Carney, and it is a shame there are not more like you."

Carney laughed.

"OK, I don't know where you did your research or who helped you come to such a glowing picture of me; maybe you asked my wife."

"I could have if you had a wife, but you do not."

"OK, Ariana, enough trickery..."

She interrupted him. "No trickery, James. You see, one of my many talents is to read people. It was what Clarant was using me for. He needed to find those he could trust implicitly, so he asked me to read people at his gatherings, to sort out the ones he could rely on. He wanted to form a group so powerful that they could run the country through a puppet PM and government. I suspected this and, although I could have left at any time, I waited until I was sure of what was happening. Then things got personal and he threatened Rex unless I did what he asked."

"And what did he ask?"

"He wanted me to be what he called his consort, but what I would call something very different."

"Why are you telling me this, Ariana? You know I am obliged to report everything you say."

"You could, James, but you won't. If you go to war against us you will lose. The alternative is for you, but only you, to have us as an ally. Be assured that although we fight a greater enemy we share your concern about the way things are developing. Especially with regard to climate change. If you keep our anonymity we will help in every way we can."

"I need to think about this."

"Yes, James, do think about it, for tomorrow, after I have helped Gregory, I will be leaving. You will only see me again if I make it so. Do not attempt to find us; it will just be a waste of public money."

Ariana walked with him down the path.

"My men, Ariana, where are they?"

"They have gone back to Clerkendale. Someone put a memory in their heads that if you were not back in five minutes they were to walk back."

"I don't believe you."

Ariana shrugged her shoulders. "Ask them, James."

He pointed his key at his car but the lights did not flash. He went over and pulled on one of the handles. Nothing. Without turning, Ariana called for Bren to unlock the car. The lights flashed and the door came open.

"Thank you, Ariana, for what I assume was a demonstration. I will meet you at Clerkendale later this morning and we will visit Gregory Clarant together."

"As you wish, James."

After the car had pulled away, they all gathered in the kitchen. Bren wanted to know how Ariana knew it was her that had jammed the locks on the car. Rosa told her that Josie had mentioned her skill. Ariana explained why she had told Carney about them.

"I did lie a little bit as I have seen the Tech team's report on Carney, but it just confirmed what I could see in him. I know it is a risk, but at the moment he is just one man. He will keep what he knows to himself until he is sure he is not being duped. I think that maybe he is even higher in the Security Services than the report on him suggests. I suspect he is head of field operations. His work with top Government advisors supports this. I want to take him to the House of the Mer. It seems to be becoming the focus of things now that Owyn has been born. We can always deal with him if doubts develop. Let's see what happens after this morning's visit."

CHAPTER 41

James Carney drove back along a lane full of cow parsley and foxgloves. He picked his men up near the gates to the estate. His questions confirmed what Ariana had said.

Am I the good man she says I am, he thought. Would I turn her into be a lab rat for the corrupt?

These questions kept going around in his mind. He said nothing to the men as he stationed them one at the front and one at the rear of the Manor.

Ariana and Rex arrived at the end of the long driveway around 11.15. Jonathan Clarant came out to meet them. He proved to be a completely different man to his brother. Ariana judged him to be sensitive and caring. His brother no doubt thought him weak, but that would have been wrong. On issues he cared about like the environment and climate change, his determination for action seemed unbending. They talked for a while about the estate and how he would have done things differently if he had been the one to inherit it.

Carney was waiting for them in the very room that Gregory had always used for his interviews with her. He was stood by the French windows looking down at a dark stain on the wooden floorboards.

"You are acquainted with Mr Carney from the Government?"

Rex smiled. "Yes, we have met before."

Ariana asked Rex if he would wait with Jonathan while she went with Carney to visit Gregory. She could sense his reluctance, but he nodded his acceptance.

Carney led her down a corridor lined with old oil paintings to a large conservatory at the rear of the building. Gregory was sat in a cane chair near the window. The glass was covered by exotic climbing plants which Ariana could not identify and which made the room dark, with only dappled light.

A faint flicker of recognition appeared in Gregory's eyes, but he remained silent.

"Has he been like this since he collapsed?"

Carney did not deny the fiction.

"Apparently so."

Ariana asked Carney to stand directly in front of him and look into his eyes. She went behind him, removed his glasses and put her hands one on each side of his head.

Carney did not take his eyes off Clarant. As Ariana worked, he thought he could see a gradual change in him. Suddenly, she dropped her hands. Clarant's head had fallen forward and now he slowly raised it to look at Carney.

"I think I know you."

Carney looked surprised. "You do, sir. I was here with Mr Yendo."

"Yendo, yes. I am sorry, I am not myself today."

Ariana had moved around into Clarant's line of sight.

"Do introduce me."

Carney turned to Ariana and then back to Gregory.

"You don't remember Ariana?"

"Ariana, so that's your name. I think if we'd met I would certainly have remembered you."

Jonathan entered the room and was surprised to find his brother talking. Gregory ignored him and acted as if little had changed.

"I think I need some rest now," he said, which was his way of dismissing them all.

Outside, Jonathan was full of relief. He could not thank Ariana enough. He talked about the possibility of a full recovery.

"You obviously brought something back to life in him. Thank you so, so much."

While Jonathan was talking to Ariana, Rex took Carney to one side.

"You must wonder why she bothered. After all, Clarant did kidnap her at gunpoint and held us here as prisoners in the basement for months."

"Kidnap?"

"It's her story and she will tell it when she wants to. Personally, I thought the man evil and the world would be better off without him, but she has changed me. Her compassion must be catching. She has asked that you come to the cottage for an evening meal tonight. You won't need your minders, so you can send them back to London. I am sure you can make an excuse for staying, if in fact a man in your position needs to make excuses. Oh, and bring some Valencian red wine, peanut butter and Marmite. We are running short."

Carney was now so curious he could not resist, and said he would be there. Rex was right: a man in his position did not have to make excuses. Now, where in this god damn rural idyll was he supposed to find Valencian wine, peanut butter and Marmite?

~

By mid afternoon word had come from the Tort Mae that they approved of Ariana's quick thinking, but they wanted reinforcements nearby from the Response team. Rosa, as the wearer of the green, overruled them. They would meet Carney and welcome him as a guest.

Carney had sent his men back and, when asked, Jonathan willingly gave him a room at the Manor for as long as he needed it. Jonathan could not wait to get back to his activism in London and see his filial duty at an end. For this, he was eternally grateful to James and Ariana.

James arrived at the cottage as the light had begun to fade. Narsin heard the car pull in and went out to help Carney with what turned out to be a box full of Valencian red from Sainsbury's.

"Welcome," he said, bowing from the waist. "We have not met before, but I know of you. As I know your name, you must know mine. I am Narsin of the moor, partner to Rosa Meldrum, whom you are about to meet."

Carney was a bit confused by the politeness of these people. It was not the modern way, but he knew that he wished it was.

When Carney walked into the kitchen-diner everyone at the table rose to greet him. Ariana thanked him for his gifts and was amused to find Rex's favourite breakfast food of Marmite and peanut butter among them.

"James, will you say a grace over our food?"

He looked confused and explained that it was not his custom.

"Never mind. I, Rosa Meldrum, will say one for you. For all that the Lord gives us, may we be truly grateful."

"Bren."

"Mother Earth, your spirits of moors and woodlands thank you for the gifts you give us."

If it was not for his earlier experiences, he would have thought he was in the hands of some nutty green group. He knew he wasn't.

They ate largely in silence, then Rosa turned to Carney.

"I am Rosa of the Tort Mae. We know who you are and wish you no harm."

"I need to know more," he replied.

"It will put you in danger. Your perceptions will be challenged. Are you prepared to accept this?"

"Yes!"

"Then, when we have finished sharing the wine you gifted us, return to London."

Ariana spoke up.

"I have given you a privilege, James. If you betray us, you know what to expect. I have asked Rosa to confirm what I feel, but we cannot be sure of you until you have faced the Mer."

"Who or what is the Mer?"

"Please trust us when we say that facing the Mer will have consequences, but none that will bring you harm. When we contact you, we will explain everything.

"Arrange two weeks' leave. You have survived the current crisis in government: you are owed it. When it is done, take a room in the town of Ilfracombe at this address. We will know when you are there."

~

James Carney was careful to drink no more than three glasses of wine. He had decided to leave the car there and collect it early the next day. He used the time walking back to the Manor to try and put his thoughts together. There was little doubt that Ariana had played with Clarant's mind. How many of them could do that and, if they could, why had they not taken over the Government to suit their own purposes? He knew that would have been a dangerous game. The public did not seem to mind being manipulated by the media, but they would quickly turn against any group they thought had a way of manipulating them by entering their heads.

Maybe they had been caught and persecuted in the past, which would account for their secrecy. He decided he would not speculate any further. He did have leave owing him and the departure of Yendo from the PM's team would give him time to take it, time he might not have when a new advisor was appointed.

He would go to Devon, see for himself how these people lived, and find out what on earth the Mer might be. One thing he felt confident about was that these people really did not wish him harm.

When he arrived early the next morning to pick up his car, he found the cottage deserted and nothing to show that Ariana and the others had been there. He checked the door and found it unlocked. Unable to resist, he went inside to look around. There was no trace of the Pixsan. Every surface had been carefully wiped. On the table was a bottle with an amateurish label naming its contents as mead wine. Next to it was a note written in a calligraphic hand. "Hope you enjoy this. We look forward to seeing you soon."

Whoever these people were, they were good, very, very good. He was actually beginning to look forward to his leave.

Chapter 42

It was a few weeks before Carney actually had his time off organised. This was his first visit to Ilfracombe, and his first sight of it from the moor pleased him. He had grown up in a small town in the Midlands. His father was a teacher and his mother a nurse. Money was tight and they lived modestly. Like any good agent, he had done his research and had come across stories about 'The Visions' which had dominated the national press for a while.

His world was at the centre of government, far from here. At this moment, he stood at the top of a steep hill lined with four-storey terraced houses. It went straight down to a small high street. Ilfracombe might as well have been a million miles from London. He was very curious about the world he was now entering.

He took his bag from the boot and locked the car. When he reached the bottom of Oxford Grove, he turned left on to the High Street. It took him a while to find the address he had been given. The numbered door was next to a restaurant that displayed a single Michelin star. He pressed the bell. There were many moments in the future when he wished he hadn't, but they were only moments.

A young girl opened the door. She looked at him curiously then enquired, "Senhor Carney?"

"Si, senhorita."

"Un momento."

The girl disappeared up the narrow staircase. It was a few minutes before an older woman appeared at the top.

"Come up, do come up. Oh, how old bones hate those stairs. Do come in, Mr Carney."

She led him into a large room that looked from the back of the building out towards the sea.

"You have an advantage over me for you know my name yet I don't know yours."

"Didn't Rosa tell you that I am her mother? Goodness, those twins; they send people here and tell us nothing. There is a sign over the restaurant door, you know, and it was me who gained us the Michelin Star."

At this stage, he decided the best thing to do was to let this woman talk. She spoke fondly of her daughters. It seemed he should know who Rosa and Tessa were. Rosa he had met, but she was not like her mother. Maybe she was like her father who was also called James, but was away at the moment learning the art of making wine from honey. Carney stayed attentive as Rosa's mother told stories of her daughters. Then, in an abrupt change to the conversation, she asked if Mr Carney was hungry.

He was. So she gave him the option of eating in the restaurant or with her. He explained that he would like to eat in the restaurant. This was his habit. He rarely cooked as he had no one to cook for. He liked to dine alone. She asked if he would come back for coffee, and he agreed. She called for Aldina, the Portuguese language student living with them, to show Mr Carney to the restaurant.

Over an excellent meal of sea bass and salads, James thought about what he had been told by Rosa's mother. On the face of it, they seemed a fairly ordinary family. One daughter had become a well-known musician, the other chose to live remotely out on the moors. What James could not work out was why he had been told to visit Rosa's mother first. Was it to show him they did not feel vulnerable, or simply to demonstrate they were no threat to anyone? After eating, he returned to the upstairs rooms. Rosa's mother gave him a front door key, explaining that she retired early as she liked to get up at six to help prepare the food for lunch. Aldina showed him to his room.

After unpacking and hanging up the few clothes he had brought with him, he decided he would take the evening air. The 'Visions' incident interested him. He realised now that the name over the restaurant door was the same as that of the two sisters who appeared in one of the reports at the time.

He walked up the hill to the old Parish Church. There was a light on inside and he could hear the sound of an organ being played. It stopped and started – indicating to James that someone was practising for Sunday. It seemed the great and good of Ilfracombe were buried in this graveyard. Large carved marble angels and Celtic crosses were dotted around among the more common stone and slate slabs showing the names of those buried beneath. As he turned the corner at the far end, he saw a young man sat on a bench looking back toward the church. When he got near, the young man turned toward him. He looked a little scruffy; he wore open-toe sandals, denims and a faded yellow T-shirt. His hair was long and he had a short, untrimmed beard.

"The bats are out."
"Bats?"
"Yes, pipistrelles."
"Oh yes, I see them now."

"Good, you are going to see many new things soon. Keep an open mind."

"I'm sorry; who are you?"

Standing, the young man answered, "I am Peter, Peter Ilfracombe. Enjoy your stay, Mr Carney."

Before James could ask how he knew his name, the man had stood up and started jogging down the slope towards the exit.

It was growing darker. The organ had gone quiet and the lights were going off in the church. It was time for him to walk back.

The next morning, he was brought from his sleep by the screaming of Herring gulls. He looked at his travel clock, and the digital display told him it was seven thirty. Picking up his wash bag and the towel that had been left for him, he crossed the hall to the bathroom. James never felt ready to face the world until he'd shaved. In the Government department where he worked, beards were still frowned upon. Some of the young field agents wore them, but he, at the age of forty-one, felt he was too old to change his ways.

He had nearly finished breakfast when Ariana entered the dining-room. Aldina nodded a hello then carried on reading the book she had open in front of her. Rosa's mother was still in the kitchen, so James asked Ariana who he should pay for his night's lodging and the meal the previous evening. Ariana laughed and told him that he was an invited guest of her people. Those invited did not pay.

On their way up to the car park, she asked him if he would let Rex drive his car. He didn't mind. Rex would probably be a much better driver than him on the narrow roads he had experienced yesterday. When they reached the car, Rex was already sat in the driving seat with Bren next to him. He didn't bother to ask how they had unlocked it. His car had a screen separating the rear from the front seats, which was not visible from the outside. This was standard in field agents' cars. Ariana apologised when she explained to James that the three tracking devices on his car had been disabled.

He expected no less and, when he pulled out his mobile phone, ostensibly to check the time, he was not surprised to find the screen black and not responding. He let it go. He was here to find out more about a 'people' that could be his country's greatest enemy or its greatest friend. Nothing he had experienced so far suggested he was in harm's way. He decided he would just relax, listen to what they had to say, and make a judgement later.

On their way to the House of the Mer, Ariana gave James a brief history of the Pixsan people. To illustrate her point, she used examples from history. Examples of where the Pixsan had tried to intervene on the side of those who valued the land and its spirits but, just as with Merlin, it had usually ended in tragedy. For centuries they had kept out of human affairs, but now two things had arisen to threaten the land. Global warming, and those who denied it, was the first, and Cernounos the second. James listened without comment as they drove on what he considered must be a circuitous route to their destination. The last part was along a narrow road with a sheer drop to one side. Trees clung to the cliffs all the way down to the sea. They finally pulled into a narrow lane on the left, then into a small clearing where some construction timbers were piled between timber stickers waiting to be moved.

As soon as the car had turned, James had a strong feeling that he should not be taking this road, but it passed as soon as he was out of the car and they were all walking down the lane. The day was bright, but a chill breeze was blowing off the sea, reminding everyone it was not quite summer yet.

When they reached the Rookery, he could see a man and a woman waiting for them. The woman had a pale complexion and long black hair like Ariana's. She was taller, but also had the same sparkling green eyes. She carried a baby in a sling in front of her. The man was thin. He had a long, straggly beard and long black hair tied in a ponytail. The man stepped forward. Bowing from the waist, he announced, "Welcome, James Carney, to the House of the Mer. My name is Corrin and this is my life partner, Charly, and Owyn our son. I must warn you that if you proceed down this path there will be consequences, but none that will bring harm from us."

He held out his hand and James took it without hesitation.

"Good. Then let us proceed."

Carney was shown to a room in the old hotel and Corrin told him to go and explore the small community. If he had any questions he could stop anyone he met and ask them. When it was time, someone would find him and call him for mid-meal. Corrin then left him to settle.

Chapter 43

It did not take long for James to find his way around. There was a pier being constructed that, when complete, looked as though it might reach along the rocks to beyond the tidal range. He could hear the noise of machinery coming from within the workshops, but he did not go in. On the other side of the combe were houses built into the rock, and in front of them a small courtyard with larger buildings. Everyone seemed to be wearing the same white clothing.

Eventually, he found his way into the Medicine Garden where Denfar was working alongside Itana. He asked about the plants and, after they had introduced themselves, Denfar explained that they all had medicinal qualities. James asked if they were gardeners. Itana laughed.

"No, we are just helping out. When the Pixsan have completed a task, they go and find somewhere else to work where they might be of help. Denfar is not needed at the moment, nor I as his amplifier, so we work here."

"So, what exactly do you do, Denfar, and what is an amplifier?"

"I am a healer, and Itana is the source of my strength when I need it."

Carney was about to ask more, but they were called to mid-meal.

He sat at the foot of the table with Ariana and Rex. Rex was asked to say grace.

He stood, saying, "Let us thank the spirits of the sea and land and the mother of the Earth for what lies before us."

Corrin spoke the grace of the Pixsan and everyone began to eat.

When the meal came to an end, Charly approached James.

"Are you afraid of the sea, James?"

"I am wary of it, but I have no fear."

"You swim, then?"

"As much as possible, for it is part of the fitness regime all agents must follow."

"I see. I will ask Corrin to fetch you a wet suit. The sea is not warm enough yet for you to swim without one."

"I am to swim in the sea?"

"Yes, and I am not sure how to explain to you what is going to happen. You see, I swim with the Mer every day. I had a Mer spirit trapped inside me when I was young. Now she swims freely beside me. We are sisters in a way; it is difficult to explain. Do not be afraid. When we enter the water I will ask them about you. One may enshroud you and let you breathe her air. Do not resist or try to hide things from them, for they are elemental creatures and I cannot predict what they will do."

Everything in James' head was telling him the whole situation was crazy. Sea spirits just did not exist. However, the tall, beautiful woman beside him talked as if this was perfectly normal. He would follow her into the sea. He was a strong swimmer. He thought he would be fine.

When they stood on the water's edge, he could make out dark shapes in the sea.

Charly turned to him.

"You can see them. They know you are here." She began to wade into the water and he followed until he felt something pull him down and enshroud him with its being.

~

"Are you alright?"

Carney had not said a word since they had come out of the sea. He had quietly changed and followed Charly to the House, where they now sat in the sitting-room overlooking the beach.

"Are you OK, Mr Carney?"

He seemed distracted and just nodded.

"The Mer found no harm in you and have offered you their friendship. They will always be visible to you now. Everyone has a Talent. Most often, it lays within them without flowering. If it does flower, it is usually in their mid teens. It is the heritage of the Pixsan, and we know how to deal with it. You are a perceptive individual, James, and this is part of your Talent. It makes you very good at your job. Now it has been fully unlocked, you can see the Talent and the conflicts in others. This is the gift or, as some would see it, the curse of the Mer. I sense I cannot help you further. I think only Meldrum the Elder can. I want Denfar and Itana to check you over then they will go with you in your car to the farm. Are you willing to do this?"

James Carney nodded.

Denfar arrived with Itana shortly afterwards. Charly met them at the door.

"I am worried about him; he seems to have shrunk inside himself. Please see what you can do."

Denfar pulled a chair to where he could sit facing James. Itana stood at his shoulder.

"Can you hear me, James?" Carney nodded. "Itana and I are going to examine you.

"You may feel strange for a few seconds. Do we have your consent?"

Carney mumbled a yes. Denfar placed his hands each side of Carney's head and drew on Itana for strength. After they had finished, Itana stayed with James while Denfar went to seek Charly. She was sitting at the kitchen table feeding the baby.

"He has a type of post traumatic stress. I imagine much of his view of the world has been challenged by his encounter with the Mer. I think you are right to send him to Meldrum the Elder. She may speed his recovery. We will take him there, but maybe it's best if Rex drives us."

"One thing more, Denfar. I have the strongest feeling that Owyn wants Tara and Rafael to be here for a while before they return to Oxford. Can you ask them?"

~

Carney's car was quite spacious, so they all fitted in easily. Denfar sat in the front next to Rex while Itana and Ariana sat either side of James. He was still saying nothing and seemed totally oblivious to what was going on around him.

After a day at the farm, there was still no change in James. Ariana tried her best, but she could not penetrate the barrier James had raised in his mind. She talked it through with Meldrum.

"Send for Denfar and Itana. I hate doing this, but I need to apply pressure to bring him back. I will need Denfar and Itana to link with me in case things go wrong. His will is strong. I must turn it to his advantage. I need to enter his mind."

~

James was unsettled and confused. He had retreated into himself and his mind had tricked him into thinking he was sitting on a beach looking out to sea. He knew they were there but he could not see them. He needed to see them. He needed to know they were real, but how could they be? No one else saw spirits in the sea. God, how he wished they were real, but thoughts of his office, his work kept crowding them out. He knew he had to choose. He would if he truly knew they were real. He felt someone calling and pushing towards him, then a presence beside him. He turned to see a rather rotund old lady dressed in white.

"Why are you fighting the Mer? They wish only to befriend you."

"You are one of them; you would not understand."

"Don't be stupid, child. I have been on this green sphere for more years than you can count. All of you Familiars are like children and, when we give you the chance to grow, what do you do? You disappear inside yourself. The Dragon Bloods lie and are corrupt. You could be part of the fight that turns the tide.

"Embrace the Mer for they are defenders of the earth and need all the allies they can get. Your choice is not complex. In your work you could help us, and always have the knowledge that we would aid you and give you sanctuary if things should go wrong. I'm sorry I can stay no longer."

James looked around to see the old lady had disappeared. He decided that he must shake off his confusion and wake up. When he did, the face of the old lady was looking down at him smiling, and Itana was next to him holding his hand.

Chapter 44

Tara and Rafael rode over to the House as soon as they received Charly's message. Corrin met them at the Rookery.

"Owyn is restless. The babe will not settle and Charly is convinced he is calling for you. Please indulge her; the women tell me the time after childbirth can be challenging, but I believe Charly is right."

Corrin headed off to the workshops, where some decisions about the pier had to be made. Tara and Rafael headed for the old hotel where they found Charly, with Owyn in her arms. She was walking up and down the sitting-room trying to settle him. He stopped wriggling as soon as they entered the room, and one of his tiny arms stretched out towards Tara. She crossed over and took him from Charly. Immediately, an image entered her mind. It was the stag in the clearing where they had met Durantia.

"He wants to go to the woods, Charly. You and Corrin must take him. You must be there when he meets with Herne in his true form. We will be with the Dryads as they circle you."

"Why did this message not come to us?"

"It seems only Owyn can truly serve two spirits. We are his bond messenger. Herne and Durantia are linked as spirits of the woods. I think Rafael and I must stay here for a while before returning to Oxford. There is no rush for me to return there, and I think I need to bond with your son like a sister would. She found a seat and settled with Owyn in her arms. The child had become quiet. Charly breathed a sigh of relief.

"It will be good to have you here. He seems to like you, so if you don't mind I will take a little time for some rest."

Tara told her to go. She and Rafael would look after Owyn until Corrin returned.

After Charly had left, Rafael and Tara sat looking out towards the sea. Owyn was sleeping quietly in Tara's arms.

"Well, Rafael, why are you looking at me like that?"

"Oh, nothing; it just occurred to me how natural you look with a baby in your arms."

"One day, perhaps, but not until this struggle with Cernounos is over."

"Perhaps this is only one battle in a long war."

"I know no more than you, Rafael, but it is said that Cernounos cannot be destroyed. Maybe the answer is sleeping in my arms. The Dryads seem to think so."

All three of them were dozing when Corrin finally returned.

Chapter 45

James Carney had been given strict instructions to stay in bed until Meldrum and Denfar had a chance to examine him again. He was sat up with his back against the wall of the rather sparse room. Orita sat beside him. He guessed her age to be no more than sixteen. She was reading aloud from a book which she explained was a synopsis of the histories of the families. He found it difficult to take it all in, but useful. The Pixsan were not some cult that invented themselves yesterday. They were truly a people with a history that went back centuries. They had managed themselves well and avoided persecution. It was certain that if they were discovered now they would end up as lab rats in the scientific institutions of the powerful. He knew the Dragon Bloods would lack compassion in their search for the secrets of the Pixsan's talents. This made their trust in him even more remarkable.

He was head of field operations for GovernmentHome Security. In putting their trust in him they were taking a hell of a risk. However, they knew immediately what he didn't. He would not betray them, even less so now, because he was becoming one of them. He had accepted the friendship of the Mer and longed to go back to their House and swim alongside Charly in the sea. He was told he could as soon as he had rested enough.

Later that day, Meldrum and Denfar decided he was fit enough to attend family-meal. When he was ready to go, Rosa and Narsin appeared in the doorway. They spoke to him for a while about how he felt, about his encounter with the Mer and what he would do now he knew of them. He was willing to swear he would never betray the Pixsan. They had the virtues the corrupt people he served lacked. He was willing to help them in any way he could.

"James, we have heard what you have to say. When you return to the House of the Mer, you will be invited to join them. Do not take this decision lightly. Believe us when we say we will take any measure necessary to protect our communities. You have been tested by the Mer and survived. If you accept the invitation, you will be one of us. If you leave, then your memory of us and your talent will be removed lest you become a servant of Cernounos. Remember – we will be working together against an enemy that would destroy us all."

James understood what they were saying. He explained that he found it difficult to fight the creeping corruption that was engulfing the Government because he felt he was on his own. Now he knew differently and would gladly accept the invitation to the House of the Mer when it was given.

When they were seated at family-meal, James was once again asked to say grace. This time he responded by thanking the Earth for all it gives.

Chapter 46

A call from Father Gary brought some disturbing news. Someone answering Dave's description had been to the Refuge in Bristol. He questioned Father Mark who was now in charge there. He was quite compelling, but as Father Mark knew nothing of the Pixsan he could tell him little. The man, almost definitely Dave, showed him a photo of a tall, thin lad dressed in tracksuit bottoms and a hoodie.

He wanted to know if the lad had been to the Refuge lately. The priest asked him why he was looking for him and received a highly dubious story about Dave being hired by his family to trace him. Father Mark explained that lots of young men came through the doors of the Refuge. Would the man give him a copy of the photo and a contact number? He promised nothing, said he would keep an eye out for the boy and give him the number if he wanted it. As soon as the man left, Father Mark took a copy of the photo and a still of the visitor from the security camera and sent them both to Father Gary.

Gary recognised the boy as the Talent sensitive, and he sent both photos on to the farm. Ariana confirmed that the man posing as a private detective was Dave. The question then became who he was working for now. Rosa and the others were in little doubt that he was in the pay of Yendo. Colin must have told Yendo about Dave, and it would not have taken long for them to make contact. Cheques would have stopped going into Dave's bank account from Clarant, so a new source of money would be welcome. There was a strong possibility that Dave would have told Yendo about the Talent sensitive and now had the job of finding him, not knowing that even if he did he would be of no use to them. There were others, though, and if Yendo knew of their existence it was unlikely he would stop until he had located one.

~

James had been improving over the last few days and was ready to go back to the House of the Mer. Rosa wanted to get as much information from him as possible before he left. He had worked closely with Yendo and would know his character. Did he know why the Prime Minister had sacked him? James explained that he had made too many enemies too quickly. He wanted to reform the Civil Service, which he considered stood in the way of progress. Government bureaucracy was conservative and disliked radical change.

Yendo had been brought into the Cabinet Office as an unelected advisor and been given powers by the PM to shake things up and bring in new people. It was not long before resistance sprung up amongst Civil Servants, and the PM soon found himself with an ultimatum: Yendo must go or his Government would be brought to a standstill. The PM felt he had no choice, and sacked his friend.

James thought Yendo an unscrupulous character who would do anything to get back at the PM. Totally unconventional, he would not have dismissed Colin's claims. If Clarant had seen something in Colin and Dave, he would follow through. He knew Clarant was not a stupid man, just one who was obsessed by money and power. This was something that Yendo shared. He guessed that Yendo's aim would be to find a Talent sensitive. With control of such a one, he could start collecting Wilds and finish the job Clarant had started.

Rosa and Narsin believed they should not delay. They must act now to stop him. If his only experience of Talent was Dave, then he would have no idea how dangerous a strong, untrained Talent could be. James was asked if he could supply them with the confidential information they needed to locate him. James agreed. He had regained his cool manner, but Rosa could detect an undercurrent of excitement. Perhaps he thought that at last he really could make a difference.

James was welcomed back to the House of the Mer by Charly. Tara was becoming like a second mother to Owyn and spent lots of time with him, allowing Charly and Corrin to do the work they needed to do in the community. Charly was instantly aware that James had lost his conflict.

"You are well, James."

"Yes."

"Your absence was noted, but even now they know you are here and will welcome you back."

"I am grateful, and I hope that the House will invite me into the community."

Charly assured him it would, but first she wanted to be sure he knew what that meant. She explained more as they walked together back towards the old hotel. Now she must feed Owyn. After, when Corrin returned, they would swim.

CHAPTER 47

Yendo had fought back against his sacking, though soon realised that, with the weight of the Civil Service against him, there was no way he was going to return to the Cabinet Office.

He did not dwell on this. There were other avenues he wanted to explore. As soon as the Home Security had finished with Colin, he picked him up and took him to his home on the outskirts of Beverly in the East Riding. From Colin, he learnt about Dave, and it did not take long to locate him. Dave convinced him that, if he could harness the talents of these people, he could bypass the normal routes to power. He needed to know more, and as soon as he learnt that Clarant's health was improving he rang Jonathan to arrange a visit.

The visit did not go well at first. Gregory was back on top of his business interests and had even travelled to London for critical votes in Parliament; however, when Yendo attempted to ask him about Ariana he was met with a blank stare and confused answers. Jonathan, who was present throughout, had decided he would not mention James and Ariana's visit. He did not trust Yendo.

Dave had been left outside on the terrace. When Yendo came out he took him to one side, making sure they were out of Jonathan's hearing. Yendo returned to Jonathan after a few minutes and asked, as it was such a fine day, if they could take a walk around the grounds before they made their return journey. No need for Jonathan to accompany them as they would leave straight after their walk. Jonathan was a little suspicious, but could see no harm in it and let them go their way.

Yendo and Dave took the circuit path, but their true aim was the copse. Dave had seen something in the woods and felt compelled by it. He felt Yendo and himself should take a closer look. As they approached the copse, Don Yendo felt the hairs on the back of his neck stand up. He was not a man to frighten easily. but there was something up ahead that made him uneasy. There seemed to be a mist forming in between the trees and they could just make out the figure of a man. Closer to, they could see he was naked and wore only a crown of branches and twigs. They tried to go further, but something was holding them back.

A voice came into Yendo's head. "There is a powerful force growing in the south. I will give you a way to find it. Power could be yours if you succeed."

As with all spirits, Cernounos could only give so much. He did not care. The only outcome he needed was human grief. If happiness and grief stayed in its normal balance he could not grow. He needed to upset that balance and, to this end, constantly sought human conflict. The victor in the conflict did not matter to him for, whoever won, someone would be left grieving. Let Yendo seek out the threat he could feel growing in the south. He would lead him to the Talent sensitive he would need.

~

Rosa had put a plan to the Tort Mae, and it had been agreed. Now she needed to travel to Bristol to see what the Response team made of it. Rex and Bren went with her. When they arrived, Rosa shared with Josie and Anna what they had learnt from James Carney. Yendo had inherited the family house from his parents. He had no siblings and had never married. The house was a medium-sized country home of the type that was once called a Gentleman's Residence. Unmodernised, it had six bedrooms but only one bathroom. It had been well maintained, but not improved. The house was surrounded by five acres of parkland.

Don Yendo had inherited enough to keep on a small staff to tend the house and gardens. He cared little about his surroundings, but knew that appearances had to be kept up for others. There were other buildings in the grounds left over from when the estate was much bigger. Yendo had restored the gamekeepers' and gardeners' cottages for guests. He hated sharing the house with anyone, apart from his elderly housekeeper.

Rosa wanted the Response team to carry out a reconnaissance mission. They would take Rex and get him as near to the house as possible. They needed to know how many Wilds Yendo had recruited and how powerful they were. The house needed to be looked at to see how secure it was. Access may be needed later to destroy documents. There was also the issue of security staff. Was Government security still in place now that Yendo had left number ten? All this was to be done as soon as possible.

Josie and Anna took little persuading. The Response team was more than ready for some action. Rosa warned caution. This had to be a professional operation. No trace must be left of their presence at or near Yendo's home. This would be their first big test.

A day later, Josie and Anna held a briefing meeting. The team would be Anna and Josie, Bren, Rex and Gerrant, the avian Talent. The Tech team had provided them with a satellite image of the ground and a map drawn up from it. All were given a task, and Rosa's message about professionalism was reinforced by Josie.

To Josie and Anna's relief, the Response team had been granted two new vehicles. It had been resisted by the traditionalists in the Tort Mae, but Rosa convinced them that a rapid Response team would not be very rapid without them. Two second-hand hybrid Toyota vans were purchased, each converted to sleep four, with plenty of storage.

They were for the exclusive use of the Response team. It was a six-hour drive to Beverly, so they would stay overnight in a campsite on the other side of Hull. The following day they would take a walk past Yendo's property. James Carney had told them that Government security had been withdrawn; they needed to check to see if he had brought in private security. They also needed to know if Yendo kept dogs. Bren could silence them if she was near enough.

The Tech team map only gave them so much information. Bren and Gerrant would pose as walkers and get as close as they could. Gerrant would get one of his birds to fly overhead to gain an accurate picture. The whole point was to get Rex close enough to see if he could feel the presence of Talent and how strong it was. They would leave the following day. Josie and Anna would travel in one van and Rex, Gerrant and Bren in the other.

Chapter 48

It was early summer and a fine day. The security guard on the gate at Leyson House, the home of Don Yendo, did not find it unusual to see two young walkers coming towards him. Bren engaged him in conversation, asking about the grounds and the house. Was it National Trust, they asked. He laughed at their supposed naiveté.

He told them a very important person lived there and it was privately owned. Just then, some dogs began to bark. The guard turned to see a buzzard drop down near the house. He told them that the bird must have spooked the dogs. They were a vicious lot and only responded to their owner. German Shepherds, he exclaimed, bred to be mean. The young couple smiled and thanked him for giving them directions. Nice young people, thought the guard as they wandered off up the road. If only all young people were polite like them.

That evening, Yendo was in the house alone. His guests were up the lane in the old cottages. He was becoming annoyed. An unexpected storm had arisen; a wind had come up out of nowhere and the dogs had been spooked twice by doors rattling in the yard.

Bren and Gerrant had taken up position near the dog kennels. Dressed in dark grey, they stood next to the walls of the stable building, where they were hard to see. The dogs started barking again, and an angry Yendo came into the yard.

"Be quiet, you mongrels. I will let you out soon enough."

He threw something into the cage which the dogs immediately began to fight over.

The cottages were just beyond the house and this was the objective for Josie, Anna and Rex. They crept along the lane, keeping in the shadow of the overhanging hawthorn. When they got near enough, Rex crept ahead. He reached out and felt a strong Response in return. Suddenly, the door to one of the cottages was flung open and a young girl could be seen running towards the house. Rex rushed back to the others.

"We have to get out of here; she is a Talent sensitive and as soon as I felt her presence she knew I was here." They retreated to the others.

Yendo rushed into the yard and tried to let the dogs out, but the kennel lock seemed to be jammed. He cursed and headed back towards the house. When he came back to the kennels with a pair of bolt cutters, everything had gone quiet and the kennel door opened with ease. Yendo would only have the word of the young Talent sensitive to tell him they were there.

The team reported back. Yendo had found his Talent sensitive. They would have to wait to see what he would do next. In the meantime, they would stay well away and let James keep them updated as to his whereabouts.

The Tort Mae sent warnings to all the communities. Most Pixsan could sense someone with Talent, although, unlike Rex, they could not gauge their strength without touching them. The majority of the Pixsan rarely left their communities, so it would be Wilds that Yendo's Talent Sensitive would most likely identify. Nevertheless, some

Pixsan had to leave their communities at times. Everyone was told to be on their guard.

~

Don Yendo was, as he would put it, pissed off. It was clear Dave could talk people into things. It hadn't worked on himself, which he put down to his own strength of character, but it clearly worked on others. Dave claimed he had been led to the girl, Ellie, but Don wasn't sure.

As far as he could see, Ellie was a skinny, mentally ill kid. No doubt she had drug problems as well, though Dave denied it. He didn't like Dave much either. A money grubber, he thought. He also had him marked as a deviant. Twice he had caught Dave trying to force himself on the girl – who could not have been older than fifteen. He had told her that if Dave tried it again she should run straight to him. God, how he hated dealing with these people.

The night of the local storm, he thought the girl had come running to him because Dave was at it again despite his warnings but, no, she was screaming about something in the yard. Something powerful. He had searched the grounds for signs of people or animals. If there had been anything, the wind would have swept it away. That puzzled him, for his neighbours had told him that there was no wind that night.

He decided that he needed to settle the girl, so he talked to her. He made it clear that he thought her special and that he would help and protect her. He moved her into the house and gave her a room next to his housekeepers. Anything she was worried about, or just wanted to talk about, she should come to him. He could not help her with her Talent, but he had gained her trust and she had bonded with him in ways he would never understand.

Yendo had made a sort of peace with his old boss. The PM hated having enemies. He knew he couldn't get Yendo back on his team, but he was happy to help him. Yendo asked for James Carney's contact details and the PM gave them. He knew Carney was continuing to observe Clarant and wanted to know what he knew. He asked him to come to Leyson House.

Yendo had no authority over Carney now, so Carney refused, saying he would consider a meeting, but now he was busy with the up-coming climate crisis talks. He would contact him when they were over. Rosa had warned him not to go near Leyson House. The Sensitive would know him as Talent, though she would not know what his Talent was. James agreed. Rosa was worried about him. He assured her he was experienced and would not put himself in danger.

Chapter 49

Tara and Charly were becoming close. Tara was spending more and more time with Owyn, and their bond had become stronger. Tara had told Corrin and Charly that Durantia had predicted this. Charly was just pleased to have Tara's help. Rafael was spending his time in the Medicine Garden where he felt completely at home. Tara suspected it might be difficult to drag him back to Oxford.

Two more weeks and their Caution would be over. Rosa had made a case to the Tort Mae for it to be shortened, and they had agreed. Itana had spent little time as their Caution and now it looked like she would miss out altogether on any fun she may have planned. Rosa was not worried. She knew Charly would sense if they had strayed. It would have produced a conflict within them. Charly assured her that they were committed to their Caution. Tara was desperate to be accepted as a true Pixsan and Rafael did not want to face the Tort Mae.

Some time passed before Tara felt Durantia's call. Family-meal was over and they were walking back with Corrin and Charly to the old hotel when Rafael and Tara's heads turned toward the woods.

"They call; now is the time. We must take Owyn to them."

They walked in silence. No sound came from the Rookery as they passed it. It was as if the woodland creatures were holding their breath. They walked through the grey light of dusk and into the clearing. Durantia was there, standing next to Herne. He was in human form and wore a green cloth garment tied and hanging from his waist. His long hair and beard melded into one around his face. Large antlers spread up from their shoulder blades. Through green eyes they stared down at the humans.

Charly lifted Owyn from the sling around her shoulders and held him up before them. To her surprise, Durantia and Herne fell on their knees before him, clasping fists over their hearts.

Into their heads came the words, "He has come to change the world, so they will try and take him from you. Do not fear. Call on us if you need to and we will turn their iron against them."

Tara looked around and she could see the shadowy shapes of the Dryads in all the trees. Herne and Durantia stood and walked away into the woods. They stopped at the edge and turned.

"You have many friends. Do not fear, for even if we fail him he will defend himself."

Rafael had worked in the woodlands of his homeland all his life. He never thought that one day he would stand among the Dryads with a life partner who called them friend. Tara's strength had taken away his fear of the spirits that had stood before them and had bowed down before the child Owyn. He was at a loss to understand what was happening, but he knew now that he was 'called' and would do whatever was necessary to defend the child.

When they returned to the old hotel, Charly voiced her concerns. Corrin and the others tried to be reassuring, but it was hard. They had all heard Herne say that they would try and take Owyn from them and that they might use iron. The House of the Mer had few defences against modern weapons. The following morning, Corrin sent a message to Rosa and Narsin. The bird arrived during first-meal. After they had eaten, they went to consult Meldrum and Konia.

Later that morning, Rosa headed up to Bristol, and Narsin rode over to the north shore to talk to Charly and Corrin. Rosa would return with members of the Response team. Leana and Bren knew what to expect, so they would lead the others. Dana, another Fire Talent, and an Earth Talent named Senaly (who shared some of Rosa's abilities), Ariana, Rex, Denfar and Itana would be permanently stationed at the Mer House.

Josie and Anna would remain with the rest of the team in Bristol to respond to developments there. If there was to be an attempt to take Owyn, then it was likely Cernounos would create distractions elsewhere. Splitting the team made sense. Josie and Anna were already accustomed to working in the city and they knew it and the surrounding areas well.

The others felt that the team they had assembled at the Mer House was strong enough to resist any attack that might come. The spirits were on their side and nobody really knew what they were capable of. Charly was reassured by all this, and she settled back into her daily routine of swimming with the Mer.

Chapter 50

In the hope of gaining more information, Yendo had travelled down to see Clarant a few times. Clarant was back to his old self when it came to business matters, but questions from Yendo about Dave or Colin just made Gregory confused, agitated and irritable.

In the end, Clarant refused to see him. On his final visit to Clerkendale, Yendo had another encounter with Cernounos. He was told that what he was looking for was on the south shore of the Severn Sea – a child so strong that it would lend him great strength. It would not be easy as the child would be protected. Force would be needed.

The compulsion in Cernounos' words made it difficult for Yendo to ignore them. He had begun planning on his way back to Yorkshire. He would return with Ellie and they would travel the shorelines of Somerset and Devon. He would rent a van and take his time exploring the coast. He had no idea how her Talent worked, but if the child was as strong as he had been told, Ellie thought she would feel its presence from quite a way off.

Yendo was worried. He had no idea what the people who held the child would be like. He did know one thing: that anyone taking a child from its family would face very strong resistance. He had two options: stealth or frontal attack with deadly force. He would decide when he thought he had enough information at his fingertips. Such was the strength of the compulsion which Cernounos had planted in his mind that he was refusing to take into account the consequences of what he was planning.

He sent Dave to Bristol to put together the team he would need should force become the chosen option. His dislike for Dave increased by the day, but he reasoned that one had to use people like Dave if goals were to be reached.

He told Ellie his plan. She was to act as if she was his daughter. She said little in response. He tried, but he could not understand her. She was as thin as a stick and as nervous as a sparrow. His housekeeper told him she only ever relaxed and ate properly when he was in the house.

Yendo did not take long to put his plan into action. Rather than hire a van, he bought a second-hand one – a small motorhome with a separate compartment for the girl. He wasn't looking forward to sharing such a small space with her. He hated sharing space with anyone, but it would be alright with Ellie. She hardly spoke and spent most of her time staring into space with eyes that never met his. They would start at Minehead and drive slowly to where the coast turned to face the Atlantic at Bull Point. The coast changed at Porlock. From there the shoreline became one of steep cliffs and narrow combes. Yendo had bought himself the most detailed maps available, although studying them gave him no clues. The area was littered with small hamlets. If you wanted to hide away, somewhere on this coastline would be a good place to do it. He would just have to put his trust in Ellie.

~

Rosa had received an encrypted mail from James Carney to let her know that Yendo had been back to see Clarant several times. His superiors were suspicious as they thought he might turn on the PM. This gave James the perfect excuse to keep a close eye on him. He knew that Yendo had bought a camper van and that he was heading south with a young girl he was calling his daughter.

Rosa let the Response team at the Mer House know. He may pass them by; it would depend on just how strong the girl's Talent was. Rex thought she might be very strong, but there was no use intervening unless they had to.

As it turned out, it was Rex who raised the alarm. He felt something on the top road and took Ariana to investigate. When they were halfway up the lane they heard an engine start and a vehicle moving off.

Corrin told them later that it was a white motorhome. It must have been Yendo and the girl. Corrin was too busy to use his birds to patrol everywhere so they sent for Gerrant, the Avian Talent. He arrived two days later and spent his days near the top road with Bren. Corrin's owls patrolled the night. The atmosphere was becoming tense at the house. They did not know what Yendo was planning, but if the spirits were right he would try and kidnap Owyn.

~

Yendo had become wary. Ellie had made him stop at the head of a combe, then told him to move on quickly. She told him the place glowed with energy. This must be the place they were looking for. He needed to get back, but not to Yorkshire. Through an Internet company, he booked an apartment in the middle of Bristol. He demanded it had more than adequate Internet. He then ordered historical and current maps of the North Devon coast to be delivered there.

The apartment was part of an old office building that had been totally renovated. It was in the middle of the city. They were met at the entrance to the underground car park by a concierge. He explained that their vehicle was too big to enter through the barriers. They were to take what they could carry and everything else would be taken up to their apartment. The vehicle would be stored safely until they needed it.

Yendo spent days studying the maps he'd had delivered, while Ellie just stood at the window staring out. He discovered the combe with the old hotel and the small inaccessible combe beside it. Old records described the tunnel between what was now the Medicine Garden and the combe of the old hotel. He looked for a satellite image but the whole area seemed just a blur. He reasoned the larger combe must house the family of the child. He would settle for a mixture of stealth and force. They were no doubt alarmed when they felt Ellie nearby, so he would leave it for a while. It would give him time to create a small team of four or five. They would wait for a calm night then head from Ilfracombe in a large dingy to the side combe. From there they would enter through the tunnel to the main combe and threaten or shoot anyone who stood in their way. Yendo never thought about failure. Those from his privileged class rarely did.

~

The Pixsan were also making plans. Rosa and Narsin had moved to the Mer House, leaving Konia and Meldrum to head the farm. Everyone had gathered in the meal room to discuss how they were going to react to the threat Yendo posed.

Above all else, the Pixsan needed to remain concealed from society. Their locations must remain anonymous. Without Cernounos, Yendo would never have located the Mer House. This posed difficulties when it came to dealing with him. Most agreed it would be foolish to try and deal with him in the outside world. He was a well known figure and another one with sudden memory loss might draw too much attention.

They would have to deal with him here at the Mer House. It was going to be risky. He would definitely come with armed support. He would have worked out that the easiest way into and out of the combe was by sea. No doubt he would take hostages to get what he wanted.

Charly was surprisingly unconcerned now by the threat Yendo posed to Owyn. She had heard the words of Herne and, as Rosa pointed out, they were hardly liable to harm the child they were so desperate to kidnap. Bren suggested that a permanent patrol be set up by the top road. Gerrant and her should be sited in the nearby woodland. Any approach would be obvious to them. Rosa disagreed. She was convinced that an attack would come by night. Anyone approaching from the road would set off the rooks and that would give them plenty of time to get Owyn to a safe place and initiate their plan of defence. Without Charly, the Mer could not differentiate one human boat from another, so it would be too risky to ask them to stop a boat from landing. Anyway, they were not sure how the Mer would react if they were told Owyn was in danger.

They needed to capture Yendo to neutralize him. They must have a patrol on both beaches. Ariana thought it most likely they would land on the beach in the side combe and come through the tunnel.

To diminish the threat of casualties, it was decided to disperse members of the community to the nearby Pixsan settlements. Most would go to the community at the head of the East Lynn water, some to the moorland farm. Only Terina from the Medicine Garden and the members of the Response team would stay with the others. They figured they would come soon. Now the waiting began.

It was a week later when they heard news from James Carney. Yendo had left Bristol for Devon. Rosa had asked one of the local fishermen, who she'd known from childhood, if he would ring her should someone come looking to hire a dingy.

Someone had, and had taken it to Watermouth Cove. It would be easy to launch it from there as the small harbour was deserted at night. The team thought it obvious that they would launch on a spring tide, which coincided with a full moon and little wind. The wind often dropped to nothing over the top of the tide. Charly had no need for fishermen's tide tables. The coming and going of the spring tides with the phases of the moon was the pattern which governed her life. They felt they could predict Yendo's arrival almost to the day – and they did come as predicted, landing in the empty combe of the Medicine Garden: Yendo, the girl and four armed men.

Yendo told one of them to stay with the boat and have it ready.

The light shone from a full moon in a cloudless sky. As they approached the tunnel, they heard a muffled cry from behind them. They turned to see the guard they had left struggling to keep hold of the rope he was trying to secure the inflatable with. Something was pulling the boat and, by the time they got back to help the guard, he had lost his grip and the inflatable dingy was heading out to sea. He motioned for silence.

Yendo wasn't worried. Always a man of caution, he had Dave stationed just a mile away in a lay-by used by walkers. He would call him once they had the child. They headed back to the tunnel. It was short enough for them not to need torches. Faint moonlight shone all around them and they could see the other beach clearly. Yendo and the girl came out first. The others followed, spreading themselves out across the beach. The old hotel loomed up before them. Just a single light shone from a doorway, and two figures came out of it, walking towards them. As they came closer, Yendo could see it was a man and a woman. The woman was tall with long black hair and wore a wetsuit, the man white trousers and a long white shirt tied at the waist. On his shoulder sat an owl. Ellie spoke quietly to Yendo.

"There are more of them we can't see."

Yendo looked around, but couldn't see anything. He started to walk toward the man and the woman. He turned and beckoned his men to follow. When he got close, he called out to the couple.

"We have come for the child. If you resist, we will kill you all."

~

The woman took the child from the sling on her back and walked toward him. He motioned for Ellie to go and fetch it from her. When Ellie had returned with the child, Yendo could see she had started to shake. He called out for his men to shoot the child's parents. Ellie screamed. "No, you have no idea what they are." No shots came and he turned to see his men a long way back, apparently frozen and unable to move.

"OK, I will do it myself; they can't come after us if they're dead." He drew a pistol and fired directly at Charly and Corrin, but a wall of sand rose up before them and fire sprung out of the beach in sheets of flame. Yendo began to scream as he felt himself sinking into the sand. Ellie sat beside him and wept. Charly emerged from the flames and took Owyn from her arms. "Come child, your conflict is deep, but the Mer will remove it."

Senaly moved between the men, picking up their weapons. They were sunk up to their knees in the sand and were struggling to get free. They had tried to fire their arms to warn Yendo, but they had been jammed by Bren. Denfar had walked behind them, covering their mouths with an evil-smelling cloth. The vapour immobilised them. Itana followed, making sure they were unconscious.

Up along the road at the lay-by, Dave sat in the van with the radio playing. Staring out through the windscreen, he thought he saw something move in the trees. It was a woman. Yes, he was sure it was a woman.

He opened the door and walked towards the woods. He could see a woman in the trees. His lucky night, he thought, until the headlights of the van came on behind him and held him in the light. He turned to see Rex leaning against the bonnet and Ariana sat in the driver's seat. Turning quickly, he started to run. Instead of getting free, he ran straight into Rafael's fist and dropped cold.

They bundled Dave into the back of the van where Ariana clasped his head between her hands and took his Talent and his memory. They drove all the way down to the beach and dumped the other four men in the back of the van. Ariana took enough of their memory for them to be totally confused about where they were that night and what they were there for. Tara and Rafael stayed. Itana and Denfar joined Rex and Ariana in the van. Denfar would keep them under while they dropped them off one at a time in different towns across the border in Somerset.

Rosa and Narsin sat with the girl Ellie in the old hotel. Rosa tried to reassure her. She just sat there looking terrified. When Corrin returned with a subdued Yendo, she visibly relaxed, but tensed again as soon as Tara and Rafael returned with Charly and Owyn. Tara told them they must go now to the clearing in the woods where Yendo must face the consequences of his actions. Yendo started to resist and shouted that he was going nowhere. Charly asked Bren to come in and Yendo yelped as he felt his hands being forced behind his back by an unknown force.

Charly turned to him.

"You have tried to take our child and threatened us with death. You have no power here. Be still and accept your punishment." Bren released him. Ellie began to shake and started to cry.

Yendo turned to her. "Don't worry, Ellie. This is all my fault; they won't harm you."

He turned to Charly. "You will not harm her, will you?"

"You ask for compassion on our part when you have shown none. Trust me when I tell you that the blood of dragons does not run through our veins. We are not blind to justice and the needs of others."

She stood and led them out of the building and onto the path toward the clearing in the woods.

As dawn approached, the light of the moon mingled with the light of dawn. The giant stag stood before them with Durantia at its shoulder.

Yendo stared in a mixture of awe and disbelief until he fell forward, lying awkwardly on the grass completely unconscious.

Durantia stepped toward them and held Tara and Ellie's hands. Tara would never forget the night she witnessed the pain that the child Ellie had suffered from the hands of men. She vowed she would help her all she could.

~

Unlike Tara, Yendo held no memories of that night. Back at home, he lay in bed drifting in and out of sleep. Apparently he had been found in an isolated spot in the Brendon Hills. His van had been there for a while when a walker found him delirious and suffering a fever. Now back in his bed, he was not sure what had happened. His housekeeper had asked him about Ellie and the men, but he just looked at her blankly.

She was pleased. She hadn't liked the girl or the men. Just trouble, she thought. The doctor called in every day. In his opinion, Don had caught a chill in the damp atmosphere of the woods where he had been found. The housekeeper did not care. He was back and would get better. If only he could find a woman who would look out for him. Ah well, she thought, she would do the best she could for now.

~

Tara talked to the others about Ellie. Perhaps she trusted Yendo because he was the first man not to have mistreated her. They could not let her back into society. Itana surprised everyone by suggesting that she and Denfar should take Ellie to live with them. Denfar had been trying to help her and, although she distrusted him at first, it seemed she was less stressed now. She was still shy of Denfar, but she told Itana that she wanted to be a healer like him. Before anything else, she would have to be taught how to heal herself. Itana had been shocked to hear from Tara that it was not just men who had played a part in her mistreatment.

James visited the following weekend to be updated. He was not surprised that Yendo had threatened their lives. He said he would have him monitored. Rosa told him there was no need: he was no longer a threat. While James was at the Mer House, a Tort Mae had been called. James swore his allegiance. It was decided that with Cernounos as an enemy and with the Familiars having computer technology to help them, they would be constantly under threat of exposure.

For centuries they had desired only to stay apart and live their lives linked to the land and its spirits. Now they needed agents among the Familiars, as threats to them could come from any quarter. James would monitor the Dragon Bloods, and Tara and Rafael the academic world. The Tech team would stay in Bristol alongside the Response team.

~

Things were settling now and Tara and Rafael had returned to the farm and their rooms over the woodshed. They sat relaxed with a glass of mead wine. It was so good to be back where they had first met. Looking at him now, she couldn't understand why she'd held him away for so long. Maybe a little bit of her did not trust men. A question she'd had in the back of her mind popped into her head.

"Rafael, when one meets a young Pixsan woman, why do they always introduce themselves with Corm in front of their names?"

Rafael laughed and took a large swig of mead from his glass.

"It dates back to the early times of the Tort Mae. After long resistance by the men and their final capitulation, the women all took the prefix Corm to their names. It is old Pixsan and roughly translates as *She who will not be led by a man*."

"I see. I think I will adopt the name CormTara."

A large cushion flew across the room toward her, which she deftly caught and aimed back at him. They tussled over it for a while until they eventually ended up in each other's arms.

~

The struggle of the Pixsan against Cernounos continues...

The author R.L Mannings can be contacted about this and other publications at:

rlmannings007@btinternet.com

https://www.amazon.co.uk/gp/product/B0BZW2CVYT/ref=dbs_a_def_rwt_hsch_vapi_tkin_p1_i0

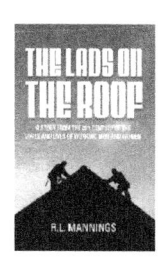

https://www.amazon.co.uk/gp/product/B0BB7VWHHM/ref=dbs_a_def_rwt_hsch_vapi_tkin_p1_i1

Printed in Great Britain
by Amazon